Marietta Holley

Poems

Marietta Holley

Poems

ISBN/EAN: 9783743463677

Manufactured in Europe, USA, Canada, Australia, Japa

Cover: Foto ©Andreas Hilbeck / pixelio.de

Manufactured and distributed by brebook publishing software (www.brebook.com)

Marietta Holley

Poems

BY

"JOSIAH ALLEN'S WIFE,"

(MARIETTA HOLLEY.)

ILLUSTRATED

BY

W. HAMILTON GIBSON,

AND OTHERS.

FUNK & WAGNALLS, Publishers.

NEW YORK :   1887.   LONDON :
18 & 20 ASTOR PLACE.   44 FLEET STREET.

DEDICATION.

WHEN I WROTE MANY OF THESE VERSES I WAS MUCH YOUNGER THAN
I AM NOW, AND THE "SWEETEST EYES IN THE WORLD" WOULD
BRIGHTEN OVER THEM, THROUGH THE READER'S
LOVE FOR ME. I DEDICATE THEM TO HER
MEMORY—THE MEMORY OF
MY MOTHER.

Contents

CONTENTS.

PREFACE.

ALL through my busy years of prose writing I have oc-
casionally jotted down idle thoughts in rhyme. Imagining
ideal scenes, ideal characters, and then, as is the way, I suppose, with more ambitious poets, trying to put myself in-
side the personalities I have invoked, trying to feel as they
would be likely to, speak the words I fancied they would
say.

The many faults of my verses I can see only too well;
their merits, if they have any, I leave with the public—which
has always been so kind to me—to discover.

And half-hopefully, half-fearfully, I send out the little
craft on the wide sea strewn with so many wrecks. But
thinking it must be safer from adverse winds because it
carries so low a sail, and will cruise along so close to the
shore and not try to sail out in the deep waters.

And so I bid the dear little wanderer (dear to me),
God-speed, and *bon voyage.*

MARIETTA HOLLEY.

NEW YORK, June, 1887.

WHAT MAKES THE SUMMER?

It is not the lark's clear tone
Cleaving the morning air with a soaring cry.
Nor the nightingale's dulcet melody all the balmy
       night—
Not these alone
Make the sweet sounds of summer;
But the drone of beetle and bee, the murmurous
       hum of the fly
And the chirp of the cricket hidden out of sight—
These help to make the summer.

Not roses redly blown,
Nor golden lilies, lighting the dusky meads.
Nor proud imperial pansies, nor queen-cups quaint and rare—
Not these alone

Make the sweet sights of summer;
But the countless forest leaves, the myriad wayside weeds
And slender grasses, springing up everywhere—
These help to make the summer.

One heaven bends above;
The lowliest head ofttimes hath sweetest rest;
O'er song-bird in the pine, and bee in the ivy low,
Is the same love, it is all God's summer;
Well pleased is He if we patiently do our best.
So hum little bee, and low green grasses grow,
You help to make the summer.

THE BROTHERS.

High on a rocky cliff did once a gray old castle stand,
From whence rough-bearded chieftains led their vassals—
    ruled the land.
For centuries had dwelt here sire and son, till it befell,
Last of their ancient line, two brothers here alone did dwell.

The eldest was stern-visaged, but the youngest smooth and
    fair
Of countenance; both zealous, men who bent the knee in
    prayer
To God alone; loved much, read much His holy word,
And prayed above all gifts desired, that they might see their
    Lord.

For this the elder brother carved a silent cell of stone,
And in its deep and dreary depths he entered, dwelt alone,
And strove with scourgings, vigils, fasts, to purify his gaze,
And sought amidst these shadows to behold the Master's face.

And from the love of God that smiles on us from bright-
    lipped flowers,
And from the smile of God that falls in sunlight's golden
    showers,

That thrills earth's slumbering heart so, where its warm rays
    fall
That it laughs out in beauty, turned he as from tempters all.

From bird-song running morn's sweet-scented chalice o'er
    with cheer,
The child's light laughter, lifting lowliest souls heaven near,
From tears and glad smiles, linked light and gloom of the
    golden day,
He counting these temptations all, austerely turned away.

And thus he lived alone, unblest, and died unblest, alone,
Save for a brother monk, who held the carvéd cross of stone
In his cold, rigid clasp, the while his dying eyes did wear
A look of mortal striving, mortal agony, and prayer.

Though at the very last, as his stiff fingers dropped the cross,
A gleam as from some distant city swept his face across,
The clay lips settled into calm—thus did the monk attest,
A look of one who through much peril enters into rest.

Not thus did he, the younger brother, seek the Master's
    face ;
But in earth's lowly places did he strive his steps to trace,
Wherever want and grief besought with clamorous com-
    plaint,
There he beheld his Lord—naked, athirst, and faint.

And when his hand was wet with tears, wrung with a grate-
ful grasp,
He lightly felt upon his palm the Elder Brother's clasp ;
And when above the loathsome couch of woe and want
bent he,
A low voice thrilled his soul, " So have ye done it unto Me."

Despised he not the mystic ties of blood, yet did he claim
The broader, wider brotherhood, with every race and
name ;
To his own kin he kind and loyal was in truth, yet still,
His mother and his brethren were all who did God's will

All little ones were dear to him, for light from Paradise
Seemed falling on him through their pure and innocent
eyes ;
The very flowers that fringed cool streams, and gemmed the
dewy sod,
To his rapt vision seemed like the visible smiles of God.

The deep's full heart that throbs unceasing 'gainst the silent
ships,
The waves together murmuring with weird, mysterious lips
To hear their untranslated psalm, drew down his anointed
ear,
And listening, lo ! he heard God's voice, to Him was he so
near.

The happy hum of bees to him made summer silence sweet,
Not lightly did he view the very grass beneath his feet,
It paved His presence-chamber, where he walked a happy
    guest,
Ah! slight the veil between, in very truth his life was blest.

And when on a still twilight passed he to the summer land,
Those whom he had befriended, weeping, clinging to his
    hand,
The west gleamed with a sudden glory, and from out the
    glow
Trembled the semblance of a crown, and rested on his brow.

And with wide, eager eyes he smiled, and stretched his
    hands abroad,
As if his dearest friend were welcoming him to his abode:
Eternal silence sealed that wondrous smile as he cried—
" Thy face! Thy face, dear Lord!" and, saying this, he died.

But legends tell that on his grave fell such a strange, pure
    light,
That wine-red roses planted thereupon would spring up
    white,
Holding such mystic healing in their cool snow bloom, that
    lain
On aching brows or sorrowful hearts, they would ease their
    pain.

A RICH MAN'S REVERIE.

The years go by, but they little seem
Like those within our dream ;
The years that stood in such luring guise,
Beckoning us into Paradise,
To jailers turn as time goes by
Guarding that fair land, By-and-By,
Where we thought to blissfully rest,
The sound of whose forests' balmy leaves
Swaying to dream winds strangely sweet,
We heard in our bed 'neath the cottage eaves.
Whose towers we saw in the western skies
When with eager eyes and tremulous lip,
We watched the silent, silver ship
Of the crescent moon, sailing out and away
O'er the land we would reach some day, some day.

But years have flown, and our weary feet
Have never reached that Isle of the Blest ;
But care we have felt, and an aching breast,
A lifelong struggle, grief, unrest,
That had no part in our boyish plans ;
And yet I have gold, and houses, and lands.

And ladened vessels a white-winged fleet,
That fly at my bidding across the sea ;
And hats are doffed by willing hands
As I tread the village street ;
But wealth and fame are not to me
What I thought that they would be.

I turn from it all to wander back
With Memory down the dusty track
Of the years that lie between,
To the farm-house old and brown,
Shaded with poplars dusky green,
I pause at its gate, not a bearded man,
But a boy with earnest eyes.

I stand at the gate and look around
At the fresh, fair world that before me lies,
The misty mountain-top aglow
With love of the sun, and the pleasant ground
Asleep at its feet, with sunny dreams
Of milk-white flowers in its heart, and clear
The tall church-spire in the distance gleams
Pointing up to the tranquil sky's
Blue roof that seems so near.

And up from the woods the morning breeze
Comes freighted with all the rich perfume

That from myriad spicy cups distils,
Loitering along o'er the locust-trees,
Scattering down the plum-trees' bloom
In flakes of crimson snow—
Down on the gold of the daffodils
That border the path below.

And the silver thread of the rivulet
Tangled and knotted with fern and sedge,
And the mill-pond like a diamond set
In the streamlet's emerald edge;
And over the stream on the gradual hill,
Its headstones glimmering palely white,
Is the graveyard quiet and still.
I wade through its grasses rank and deep,
Past slanting marbles mossy and dim,
Carven with lines from some old hymn,
To one where my mother used to lean
On Sunday noons and weep.
That tall white shape I looked upon
With a mysterious dread,
Linking unto the senseless stone
The image of the dead—
The father I never had seen;
I remember on dark nights of storm,
When our parlor was bright and warm,
I would turn away from its glowing light,

And look far out in the churchyard dim,
And with infinite pity think of him
Shut out alone in the dismal night.

And the ruined mill by the waterfall,
I see again its crumbling wall,
And I hear the water's song.
It all comes back to me—
Its song comes back to me,
Floating out like a spirit's call
The drowsy air along;
Blending forever with my name
Wonderful prophecies, dreamy talk,
Of future paths when I should walk
Crowned with manhood, and honor, and fame.

I shut my eyes and the rich perfume
Of the tropical lily fills the room
From its censer of frosted snow;
But it seems to float to me through the night
From those apple-blossoms red and white
That starred the orchard's fragrant gloom;
Those old boughs hanging low,
Where my sister's swing swayed to and fro
Through the scented aisles of the air;
While her merry voice and her laugh rung out
Like a bird's, to answer my brother's shout,
As he shook the boughs o'er her curly head,

Till the blossoms fell in a rosy rain
On her neck and her shining hair.
Oh, little Belle !
Oh, little sister, I loved so well;
It seems to me almost as if she died
In that lost time so gay and fair,
And was buried in childhood's sunny plain;
And she who walks the street to-day,
Or in gilded carriage sweeps through the town
Staring her humbler sisters down,
With her jewels gleaming like lucent flame,
Proud of her grandeur and fine array,
Is only a stranger, who bears her name.

And the little boy who played with me,
Hunting birds'-nests in sheltered nooks,
Trudging at nightfall after the cows,
Exploring the barn-loft, fording the brooks,
  ending, in school-time, puzzled brows
Over the same small lesson books ;
Who knelt by my side in the twilight dim,
Praying " the Lord our souls to keep,"
Then on the same pillow fell asleep,
Hushed by our mother's evening hymn ;
Whose heart and mine kept such perfect time,
Such loving cadence, such tender rhyme,
Blent in child grief, and perfected in glee—

We meet on the street and we clasp the hand,
And our names on charitable papers stand
Side by side, and we go and bow
Our two gray heads with prayer and vow,
In the same grand church, and hasty word
Of anger, has never our bosoms stirred.
Yet a whole wide world is between us now ;
How broad and deep does the gulf appear
Between the hearts that were so near !

I have pleasure grounds and mansions grand,
Low-voiced servants come at my call,
From Senate my name sounds over the land
In "ayes" and "nays" so solemnly read ;
They call me " Honorable," " General," and all,
But to-night I am only Charley again,
I am Charley, and want to lay my head
On my mother's heart and rest,
With her soft hand pressed upon my brow
Curing its weary pain.
But never, nevermore will it be,
For mould and marble rises now
Between my head and that loving breast ;
And death has a cruel power to part—
Forever gone and lost to me
That true and tender heart.

Oh, mother, I've never found love like thine,
Never have eyes looked into mine
With such proud love, such perfect trust.
Never have hands been so true and kind,
To lead me into the path of right—
Hands so gentle, and soft, and white,
That on my head like a blessing lay.
And led me a child and guided my youth ;
To-night 'tis a dreary thought, in truth,
That those gentle hands are dust.
That I may be blamed, and you not be sad,
That I may be praised, and you not be glad ;
'Tis a dreary thought to your boy to-night,
That over your sweet smile, over your brow,
The clay-cold turf is pressing now,
That never again as the twilight falls
You will welcome your boy to the old brown walls
Of the homestead far away.

The homestead is ruined—gone to decay,
But we read of a house not made with hands,
Whose firm foundation forever stands;
And there is a twilight soft and sweet.
Will she not stand with outstretched hands
My homesick eyes to meet—
To welcome her boy as in days before,
To home, and to rest, forevermore ?

But the years come and the years go,
And they lay on her grave as they silently pass,
Red summer buds and wreaths of snow,
And springing and fading grass.
And far away in an English town,
In the secluded, tranquil shade
Of an old Cathedral quaint and brown,
Another grave is made—
A small grave, yet so high
It shadowed all the world to me.
And darkened earth and sky.
But only for a time; it passed.
The unreasoning agony,
Like a cloud that drops its rain;
And light shone into our hearts at last,
And patience born of pain.
And now like a breath of healing balm
The sweet thought comes to me,
That my child has reached the Isle of Calm,
Over the silent sea—
That my pure little Blanche is safe in truth,
Safe in immortal beauty and youth.

When she left us in the twilight gloom,
When she left her empty nest,
And the aching hearts below;
Full well, full well I know,

What tender-eyed angel bent
Down for my brown-eyed little bird,
From the shining battlement.
I know with what fond caressing,
And loving smile and word,
And look of tender blessing,
She took her to her breast,
And led her into some quiet room,
In the mansions of the blest.
Oh, mother, beloved, oh, child so dear,
Not by a wish, would I lure you here.

My son is a bright, brave boy, with a grace
Of beauty caught from his mother's face,
And his mother and he in truth are dear,
Full tenderly, and fond, and near
My heart is bound to my wife and child;
But the summer of life is not its May,
And dreams and hopes that our youth beguiled,
Are but pallid forms of clay.

There's the boy's first love and passionate dream.
A face like a morning star, a gleam
Of hair the hue of a robin's wing—
Brown hair aglow with a golden sheen,
And eyes the sweetest that ever were seen.

Mary, we have been parted long,
You were proud, and we both were wrong,
But 'tis over and past, no living gleam
Can come again to the dear, dead dream.
It is dead, so let it lie,
But nothing, nothing can ever be
Like that old dream to you or to me.

I think we shall know, shall know at last,
All that was strange in all the past,
Shall one day know, and shall haply see
That the sorrows and ills, that with tears and sighs,
We vainly endeavored to flee,
Were angels who, veiled in sorrow's guise
Came to us only to bless.
Maybe we shall kneel and kiss their feet,
With grateful tears, when we shall meet
Their unveiled faces, pure and sweet,
Their eyes' deep tenderness.
We shall know, perchance, had these angels come
Like mendicants unto a kingly gate
When we sat in joy's royal state,
We had barred them from our home.
But when in our doorway one appears
Clothed in the purple of sorrow's power,
He will enter in, no prayers or tears
Avail us in that hour.

So what we call our pains and losses
We may not always count aright,
The rough bars of our heavy crosses
May change to living light.

GLORIA THE TRUE.

GAYLY a knight set forth against the foe,
For a fair face had shone on him in dreams ;
A voice had stirred the silence of his sleep,
" Go win the battle, and I will be thine."

So, for the love of those appealing eyes,
Led by low accents of fair Gloria's voice,
He wound the bugle down his castle's steep,
And gayly rode to battle in the morn.

And none were braver in the tented field,
Like lightning heralding the doomful bolt :
The enemy beheld his snowy plume,
And death-lights flashed along his glancing spear.

But in the lonesome watches of the night,
An angel came and warned him with clear voice,
Against high God his rash right arm was raised,
Was rashly raised against the true, the right.

He strove to drown the angel voice with song
And merry laughter with his princely peers ;
But still the angel bade him with clear voice,
" Go join the ranks you rashly have opposed."

" Oh, Angel !" cried he, " they are few and weak,
They may not stand before the press of knights;"
But still the angel bade him with clear voice,
" Go help the weak against the mighty wrong."

At last the words sunk deep within his heart,
With god-like courage cried he out at last,
" Oh, Gloria, beautiful, I can lose thee,
Lose life and thee, to battle for the right."

And when he joined the brave and stalwart ranks,
Like Saul amid his brethren he stood,
Braver and seemlier than all his peers,
And nobly did he battle for the right.

Gentlest unto the weak, and in the fray,
So dauntless, none—no fear of man had he;
He wrought dismay in Error's blackened ranks
So nobly did he battle for the right.

But at the last he lay on a lost field ;
Couched on a broken spear, he pallid lay;
With dying lips he murmured Gloria's name,
" The field is lost, and thou art lost to me."

When, lo! she stood beside him, pure and fair,
With tender eyes that blessed him as he lay;
And, lo! she knelt and clasped his dying hands,
And murmured, " I am thine, am thine at last."

With wondering eyes, he moaned, " All—all is lost,
And I am dying." " Ah, not so," she cried,
" Nothing is lost to him who dare be true;
Who gives his life shall find it evermore."

" Methought I saw the spears beat down like grain,
And the ranks reel before the press of knights :
The level ground ran gory with our wounds ;
Methought the field was lost, and then I fell."

" Be calm," she cried, " the right is never lost,
Though spear, and shield, and cross may shattered be,
Out of their dust shall spring avenging blades
That yet shall rid us of some giant wrong.

" And all the blood that falls in righteous cause,
Each crimson drop shall nourish snowy flowers
And quicken golden grain, bright sheaves of good,
That under happier skies shall yet be reaped.

" When right opposes wrong, shall evil win ?
Nay, never—but the year of God is long,
And you are weary, rest ye now in peace,
For so He giveth His beloved sleep."

He smiled, and murmured low, " I am content,"
With blissful tears that hid the battle's loss ;
So, held to her true heart he closed his eyes,
In quietest rest that ever he had known.

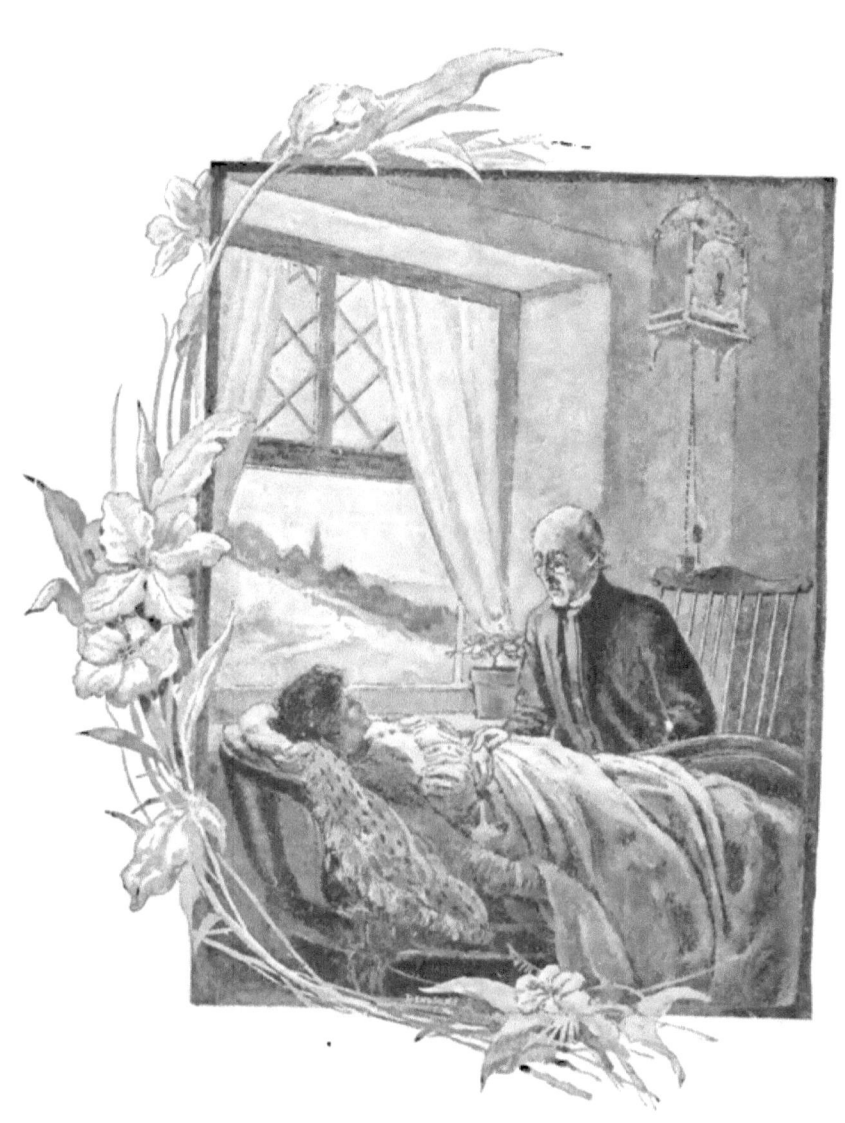

THE DEACON'S DAUGHTER.

THE spare-room windows wide were raised,
 And you could look that summer day
On pastures green, and sunny hills,
 And low rills wandering away.
Near by, the square front yard was sweet
 With rose and caraway.

Upon a couch drawn near the light,
 The Deacon's only daughter lay,
Bending upon the distant hills
 Her eyes of dark and thoughtful gray;
The blue veins on her forehead shone
 'Twas wasted so away.

She moved, and from her slender hand
 Fell off her mother's wedding-ring:
She smiled into her father's face—
 " So drops from me each earthly thing;
My hands are free to hold the flowers
 Of the eternal spring."

She had ever walked in quiet ways,
 Not over beds of flowery ease,

But Sundays in the village choir
   She sweetly sang of " ways of peace,"
Of " ways of peace and pleasantness,"
   She trod such paths as these.

No sweeter voice in all the choir
   Praised God in innocence and truth,
The Deacon in his straight-backed pew
   Had dreams of her he lost in youth,
And thought of fair-faced Hebrew maids—
   Of Rachel, and of Ruth.

But she had faded, day by day,
   Growing more mild, and pure, and sweet,
As nearer to her ear there came
   A distant sea's mysterious beat,
Till now this summer afternoon,
   Its waters touched her feet.

Upon the painted porch without
   Two women stood, and whispered low,
They thought " she'd go out with the day,"
   They said, " the Deacon's wife went so,"
And then they gently pitied him--
   " It was a dreadful blow,"

" But she was good, she was prepared,
   She would be better off than here,"

And then they thought " 'twas strange that he,
　Her father, had not shed a tear,"
And then they talked of news, and all
　The promise of the year.

Her father sat beside the bed,
　Holding her cold hands tenderly,
And to the everlasting hills
　He mutely turned his eyes away :
" My God, my Shelter, and my Rock,
　Oh shadow me to-day!"

He knew not when she crossed the stream,
　And passed into the land unseen,
So gently did she go from him
　Into its pastures still and green ;
Into the land of pure delight,
　And Jordan rolled between.

Then knelt he down beside his dead,
　His white locks lit with sunset's flame :
" My God! oh leave me not alone—
　But blessed be Thy holy name."
The golden gates were lifted up
　The King of Glory came.

SONGS OF THE SWALLOW.

SPRING.

THE sides of the hill were brown, but violet buds had started
   In gray and hidden nooks o'erhung by feathery ferns and
      heather,
And a bird in an April morn was never lighter-hearted
   Than the pilot swallow we saw convoying sunny weather,
And sunshine golden, and gay-voiced singing-birds into the
      land ;
   And this was the song—the clear, shrill song of the
      swallow,
That it carolled back to the southern sun, and his brown
      winged band,
   Clear it arose, " Oh, follow me—come and follow—and
      follow."

A tender story was in his eyes, he wished to tell me I knew,
   As he stood in the happy morn by my side at the garden-
      gate ;
But I fancy the tall rose branches that bent and touched his
      brow,
   Were whispering to him, " Wait, impatient heart, oh,
      wait,

Before the bloom of the rose is the tender green of the leaf ;
   Not rash is he who wisely followeth patient Nature's ways,
The lily-bud of love should be swathed in a silken sheaf,
   Unfolding at will to summer bloom in the warm and per-
      fect days."

So silently sailed the early sun, through clouds of fleecy
   white ;
   So stood we in dreamy silence, enwrapped in a tender
      spell ;
But the pulses of soft Spring air were quickened to fresh
   delight,
   For I read in his eye the story sweet, he longed, yet feared
      to tell ;
It spoke from his heart to mine, and needed no word from
   his mouth,
   And high o'er our heads rang out the happy song of the
      swallow ;
It cried to the sunshine and beauty and bloom of the South,
   Exultingly carolling clear, " Oh, follow me—oh, follow."

———

SPRING SONG OF THE SWALLOW.

Oh, the days are growing longer ;
So rang the jubilant song of the swallow ;
I come a-bringing beauty into the land,

The sky of the West grows warm and yellow,
  Oh, gladness comes with my light-winged band,
    And the days are growing longer.

Oh, the days are growing longer,
The wavy gleam of our fluttering wings,
  Touching the silent earth so lightly,
Will wake all the sleeping, beautiful things,
  The world will glow so brightly—brightly ;
    And the days are growing longer.

Oh, the days are growing longer,
All the rivulets dumb will laugh, and run
  Over the meadows with dancing feet :
Following the silvery plough of the sun,
  Will be furrows filled with wild flowers sweet ;
    And the days are growing longer.

Oh, the days are growing longer :
Over whispering streams will rushes lean,
  To answer the waves' soft murmurous call ;
The lily will bend from its watch-tower green,
  To list to the lark's low madrigal,
    And the days are growing longer.

Oh, the days are growing longer :
When they lengthen to ripe and perfect prime,
  Then, oh, then, I will build my happy nest :

And all in that pleasant and balmy time,
 There never will be a bird so blest ;
  And the days are growing longer.

SUMMER.

Now sinks the Summer sun into the sea :
 Sure never such a sunset shone as this,
 That on its golden wing has borne such bliss ;
  Dear Love to thee and me.

Ah, life was drear and lonely, missing thee,
 Though what my loss I did not then divine :
 But all is past—the sweet words, thou art mine,
  Make bliss for thee and me.

How swells the light breeze o'er the blossoming lea,
 Sure never winds swept past so sweet and low,
 No lonely, unblest future waiteth now :
  Dear Love for thee and me.

Look upward o'er the glowing West, and see,
 Surely the star of evening never shone
 With such a holy radiance—oh, my own,
  Heaven smiles on thee and me.

SUMMER SONG OF THE SWALLOW.

You will journey many a weary day and long,
  Ere you will see so restful and sweet a place,
As this, my home, my nest so downy and warm,
  The labor of many happy and hopeful days;
But its low brown walls are laid and softly lined,
  And oh, full happily now my rest I take,
And care not I when it lightly rocks in the wind,
    For the branch above though it bends will never
      break ;
And close by my side rings out the voice of my mate—
      my lover ;
Oh, the days are long, and the days are bright—and
    Summer will last forever.

Now the stream that divides us from perfect bliss
  Seems floating past so narrow—so narrow,
You could span its wave such a morn as this,
  With a moment winged like a golden arrow,
And the sweet wind waves all the tasselled broom,
  And over the hill does it loitering come,
Oh, the perfect light—oh, the perfect bloom,
  And the silence is thrilled with the murmurous hum
Of the bees a-kissing the red-lipped clover ;
Oh, the days are long, and the days are bright—and
    Summer will last forever.

When the West is a golden glow, and lower
  The sun is sinking large and round,
Like a golden goblet spilling o'er,
  Glittering drops that drip to the ground—
Then I spread my lustrous wings and cleave the air
  Sailing high with a motion calm and slow,
Far down the green earth lies like a picture fair.
  Then with rapid wing I sink in the shining glow :
A-chasing the glinting, gleaming drops ; oh, a diver
Am I in a clear and a golden sea, and Summer will last
    forever.

The leaves with a pleasant rustling sound are stirred
  Of a night, and the stars are calm and bright :
And I know, although I am only a little bird,
  One large serious star is watching me all the night.
For when the dewy leaves are waved by the breeze,
  I see it forever smiling down on me.
So I cover my head with my wing, and sleep in peace,
  As blessed as ever a little bird can be ;
And the silver moonlight falls over land and sea and
    river,
And the nights are cool, and the nights are still, and
    Summer will last forever.

I think you would journey many and many a day,
  Ere you so contented and blest a bird would see :

Not all the wealth of the world could lure my love away,
　For my brown little nest is all the world to me ;
And care not I if brighter bowers there are
　　Lying close to the sun—where tall palms pierce the
　　　sky ;
Oh, you would journey a weary way and a far,
　Ere you would behold a bird so blest as I ;
And singing close to my side is my mate—my king—
　　my lover ;
Oh, the days are long, and the days are bright—and
　　Summer will last forever.

AUTUMN.

Yes! yes! I dare say it is so,
And you should be pitied, but how could I know,
Watching alone by the moon-lit bay ;
But that is past for many a day,
For the woman that loved, died years ago,
　　　　　Years ago.

She had loving eyes, with a wistful look
In their depths that day, and I know you took
Her face in your hands and read it o'er,
As if you should never see it more ;
You were right, for she died long years ago,
　　　　　Years ago.

Had I trusted you—for trust, you know
Will keep love's fire forever aglow;
Then what would have mattered storm or sun,
But the watching—the waiting, all is done;
For the woman that loved, died years ago,
        Years ago.

Yes; I think you are constant, true and good,
I am tired, and would love you if I could;
I am tired, oh, friend, tired out; and yet,
Can we make sweet morn of the dim sunset?
The woman that loved, died years ago,
        Years ago.

Not a pulse of my heart is stirred by you,
No; even your tears cannot move me now;
So leave me alone, what is said is said,
What boots your prayers, she is dead! is dead!
The woman you loved, long years ago,
        Years ago.

AUTUMN SONG OF THE SWALLOW.

The sky is dark and the air is full of snow,
  I go to a warmer clime afar and away;
Though my heart is so tired I do not care for it now,

But here in my empty nest I cannot stay;
　　　　Thus cried the swallow,
I go from the falling snow, oh, follow me—oh, follow.

One night my mate came home with a broken wing,
　　So he died; and my brood went long ago;
And I am alone, and I have no heart to sing,
　　With no one to hear my song, and I must go;
　　　　Thus cried the swallow,
Away from dust and decay, oh, follow me—oh, follow.

But I think I will never find so warm and safe a nest,
　　As my home, in the pleasant days gone by, gone by,
I think I shall never fold my wings in such happy rest,
　　Never again—oh, never again till I die;
　　　　Thus cried the swallow,
But I go from the falling snow, oh, follow me—oh, follow.

THE COQUETTE.

How can I be to blame ?
  Is it my fault I am fair ?
I did not fashion my features,
  Or brush the gold in my hair ;
Because my eyes are so blue and bright,
  Must I never look up from the ground,
But put out with my eyelids' snow their light,
  Lest some foolish heart they should wound ?

How can I be in fault ?
  I am sure where hearts are so few,
It is difficult to discern
  The diamonds of paste from the true ;
I thought him like all the rest,
  Skilful in playing his part ;
As careful at cards or at chess,
  As winning a woman's heart.

I am sure it is nothing wrong,
  Nothing to think of—and yet
I know I lured him with glance and song,
  Into my shining net ;

Provokingly cold at first he seemed,
  Like crystal to smiles and sighs,
But at last he felt the magic that gleamed
  In my dreamy violet eyes.

And I led him on and on,
  Farther, in truth, than I strove.
For he frightened me with the earnestness
  And violence of his love ;
These calm-eyed men deceive—
  Had I known the man had a heart,
I would have paused, I would, I believe,
  Have acted a different part.

In his royal indignation
  He uttered some wholesome truth—
He almost roused the emotion
  That died in my innocent youth ;
Emotion that lived when life was new,
  Ere that man my pathway crossed,
Who played me a game untrue,
  When I staked all my love, and lost.

Oh for a saintly beauty,
  What efforts my soul did make ;
I thought all goodness and purity
  Were possible for his sake ;

The world seemed born anew, my life
  Such holy meaning wore,
I fancy so fair and fond a dream
  Never fell into ruins before.

He toyed with my fresh affection
  As he breathed the country air,
To refresh him after a season
  Of fashion, and falsehood, and glare :
Had he not slain my tenderness,
  Had my life been more sweet,
I might have known nobler happiness
  Than to humble men to my feet.

But now I love to lure them on,
  To make them slaves to my gaze,
Like serfs to a conqueror's chariot,
  Like moths to a candle-blaze.
I melt most royally time, the pearl,
  And quaff the cup like a queen,
And forget in the dizzy tumult and whirl,
  The woman I might have been.

LITTLE NELL.

Clasp your arms round her neck to-night,
    Little Nell,
Arms so delicate, soft and white,
And yet so strong in love's strange might ;
Clasp them around the kneeling form,
Fold them tenderly close and warm,
      And who can tell
But such slight links may draw her back,
Away from the fatal, fatal track :
      Who can tell,
      Little Nell ?

Press your lips to the lips of snow,
      Little Nell ;
Oh baby heart, may you never know
The anguish that makes them quiver so :
But now in her weakness and mortal pain,
Let your kisses fall like a dewy rain,
      And who can tell
But your innocent love, your childish kiss
May lure her back from the dread abyss ;
      Who can tell,
      Little Nell.

Lay your cheek on her aching breast,
    Little Nell ;
To you 'tis a refuge of holy rest,
But a dying bird never drooped its crest
With a deadlier pain in its wounded heart ;
Ah ! love's sweet links may be torn apart,
    Little Nell ;
The altar may flame with gems and gold,
And splendor be bought, and peace be sold,
      But is it well,
    Little Nell ?

Veil her face with your tresses bright,
    Little Nell ;
Hide that vision out of her sight—
Those dark dark eyes with their tender light—
Uplift your pure face, can it be
She will bid farewell to heaven and thee,
    Little Nell ?
No ; your mute lips plead with eloquent power,
Her tears fall like a tropic shower ;
      All is well,
    Little Nell.

Close your blue eyes now in sleep,
    Little Nell ;
Her angel smiles to see her weep ;

At morn a ship will cleave the deep,
And one alone will be borne away,
And one will clasp thee close, and pray :
    Oh Little Nell,
Never, never beneath the sun,
Will you dream what you this night have done.
    Done so well,
    Little Nell.

THE FISHER'S WIFE.

A LONG, low waste of yellow sand
Lay shining northward far as eye could reach,
Southward a rocky bluff rose high
Broken in wild, fantastic shapes.
Near by, one jagged rock towered high,
And o'er the waters leaned, like giant grim,
Striving to peer into the mysteries
The ocean whispers of continually,
And covers with her soft, treacherous face.
For the rest, the sun was sinking low
Like a great golden globe, into the sea ;
Above the rock a bird was flying
In dizzy circles, with shrill cries,
And on a plank floated from some wreck,
With shreds of musty seaweed
Clinging to it yet, a woman sat
Holding a child within her arms ;
A sweet-faced woman—looking out to sea
With dark, patient eyes, and singing to the child.
And this the song she in the sunset sang :

Thine eyes are brown, my beauty, brown and bright,
  Drowned deep in languor now, the angel Sleep

Is clasping thee within her arms so white,
  Bearing thee up the Dreamland's sunny steep.
       Oh, baby, sleep, my baby, sleep.

Thy father's boat, I see its swaying shroud
  Like a white sea-gull, swinging to and fro
Against the ledges of a crimson cloud,
  A tiny bird with flutt'ring wing of snow.
       Oh, baby, sleep, my baby, sleep.

Thy father toils beyond the harbor bar,
  And, singing at his toil, he thinks of thee:
Lit by the red lamp of the evening star
  Home will he come, will come to thee and me.
       Oh, baby, sleep, my baby, sleep.

His cabin shall be bright with flowers sweet,
  The table shall be set, the fire shall glow.
We'll wait within the door, his coming steps to greet,
  And if my eye be sad, he will not know—
       Oh, baby, sleep, my baby, sleep.

He will not pause to ponder things so slight,
  He is not one a smile to prize or miss;
Yet he would shield us with a strong arm's might,
  And he will meet us with a loving kiss—
       Oh, baby, sleep, my baby, sleep.

But would I could forget those other days
  When if with gayer gleam mine eyes had shone,
Or shade of sorrow, gentlest eyes would gaze
  With tender questioning into my own.
          Oh, baby, sleep, my baby, sleep.

Thine eyes are brown—thou hast thy father's eyes,
  But those, my darling, those were clear and blue.
Ah, me! how sorrowfully that sea-bird cries,
  Cries for its mate, oh, tender bird and true;
          My baby, sleep, my baby, sleep.

Oh, of my truest love well worthy he,
  And near was I, ah, nearest to his heart;
But ships are parted on the dreary sea
  Swept by the waves, forever swept apart—
          Oh, baby, sleep, my baby, sleep.

And sometimes sad-eyed women sighing say,
  Sweet love is lost, all that remains is rest,
So in their weakness they are lured to lay
  Their head upon some strong and loving breast.
          Oh, baby, sleep, my baby, sleep.

  *   *   *   *   *   *

Our cabin stands upon the dreary sands,
  And it is sad to be alone, alone.
But on my bosom thou hast lain thy hands,
  Near to me art thou, near, my precious one—
          My baby, sleep, my baby, sleep.

The red light faded as she sung,
A chill breeze rose and swept across the sea,
She drew her cloak still closer round the child,
And turned toward the cabin;
As she went a faint glow glimmered
In the east, and slowly rose—
The silver crescent of the moon.
Another, paler light, than the warm sunset glow,
But clear enough to guide her home.

THE LAND OF LONG AGO.

Now while the crimson light fades in the west,
  And twilight drops her purple shadows low—
We stand with Memory on the mountain's crest,
  That overlooks the land of Long Ago.

Unmoved and still the form beside us stands,
  While mournful tears our heavy eyes o'erflow,
As silently he lifts his shadowy hands,
  And points us to the land of Long Ago.

It lies in beauty 'neath our sad eyes' range,
  Bathed in a richer light, a warmer glow;
For fairer moons, and sunsets rare and strange,
  Illume the landscape of the Long Ago.

We see its vales of peace, its hills of light
  Shine in the rosy air, ah! well we know—
That nevermore will bless our yearning sight,
  So fair and dear a land as Long Ago.

We see the gleaming spires of those high halls
  We garnished with bright gems and precious show;
No foot within the gilded doorway falls,
  Empty the rooms within the Long Ago.

Troops of white doves still haunt the shining towers,
   And fold in blissful calm, their wings of snow :
We bade them build their nests in brighter bowers,
   But still they linger in the Long Ago.

There in its sunny bay stand stately ships,
   We freighted for fair lands where we would go ;
Still gleams our gold within their secret crypts,
   Becalmed beside the shore of Long Ago.

Between that land and this of dread and doubt,
   The silent years have drifted trackless snow ;
Hiding the pathway where we wandered out,
   Forever from the land of Long Ago.

LEMOINE.

In the unquiet night,
With all her beauty bright,
  She walketh my silent chamber to and fro;
Not twice of the same mind,
Sometimes unkind—unkind,
  And again no cooing dove hath a voice so sweet and low.

Such madness of mirth lies
In the haunting hazel eyes,
  When the melody of her laugh charms the listening
      night;
Its glamour as of old
My charméd senses hold,
  Forget I earth and heaven in the pleasures of sense and
      sight.

With sudden gay caprice
Quaint sonnets doth she seize,
  Wedding them unto sweetness, falling from crimson lips;
Holding the broidered flowers
Of those enchanted hours,
  When she wound my will with her silk round her white
      finger-tips.

Then doth she silent stand,
Lifting her slender hand,
　　On which gleams the ring I tore from his hand at Bay-
　　　　wood ;
The tiny opal hearts
Are broken in two parts,
　　And where the ruby burned there hangeth a drop of
　　　　blood.

Then with my burning cheek,
Raising my head, I speak,
　　" Lemoine, Lemoine, my lost !　Oh, speak to me once, I
　　　　pray !"
But no word will she deign,
Adown the shining lane,
　　The long and lustrous lane of the moonlight she glides
　　　　away.

I fancy oft a stir,
Of wings seem following her,
　　Trailing a terrible gloom along the oaken floor,
As she walks to and fro ;
Louder the strange sounds grow
　　To a nameless, dreadful horror, that floods the chamber
　　　　o'er.

And then I raise my head
From terror-haunted bed,

And hush my breath, and my very pulses hush and hark ;
But as I glance around,
The stir, the murmuring sound,
  Dies away in the moonlight, lying there stiff and stark.

And thus you ever flee,
Elude and baffle me,
  My lady you will not always so lightly glide away;
Though on the swiftest breeze,
You sail o'er farthest seas,
  Remember, side by side we two will stand one day.

Though my dust feed the wind,
Yours be with prayer consigned
  To the keeping of churchyard seraphs and marble saints :
Lemoine, we two shall meet,
And not then at my feet
  Will you fetter a late repentance with wiles and tearful
      plaints.

Repentance deep and strong,
That would have found a tongue,
  And shrieked the truth to heaven with madd'ning din :
The truth of that dread hour,
That black accursed hour,
  When to free you from hated fetters, I plunged my soul
      in sin.

Whatever wise man thinks,
Sin forges strongest links,
    You can break them never, although for a time you may
        hide
Buried in flowers and wine;
This chain of thine and mine,
    At the last dread day of doom will draw us side by side.

If one, then both are cursed,
And come the best, the worst,
    Forever and ever your fate and mine are entwined :
And though it be mad—mad,
Heaven knows the thought is glad,
    I do not breed my thoughts, how can I help my mind.

———

So silent doth she come,
Standing here pale and dumb,
    With her finger laid on her lips in a warning way ;
Her dark eyes looking back,
As if upon her track
    And mine, some phantom shape of impending evil lay.

But when I strive to see,
Of what she's warning me,
    Cruelly calm, no sign will she deign to love or fears ;
Unheeding vow or prayer,
As noiseless as the air,
    She glideth into the pallid moonlight and disappears.

SLEEP.

Come to me soft-eyed sleep,
   With your ermine sandalled feet :
Press the pain from my troubled brow
   With your kisses cool and sweet ;
Lull me with slumbrous song,
   Song of your clime, the blest,
While on my heavy eyelids
   Your dewy fingers rest.

Come with your native flowers,
   Heartsease and lotus bloom,
Enwrap my weary senses
   With the cloud of their perfume ;
For the whispers of thought tire me,
   Their constant, dull repeat,
Like low waves throbbing, sobbing,
   With endless, endless beat.

THE LADY MAUD.

I sit in the cloud and the darkness
  Where I lost you, peerless one;
Your bright face shines upon fairer lands,
  Like the dawning of the sun,
And what to you is the rustic youth,
  You sometimes smiled upon.

You have roamed through mighty cities,
  By the Orient's gleaming sea,
Down the glittering streets of Venice,
  And soft-skied Araby;
Life to you has been an anthem,
  But a solemn dirge to me.

For everywhere, by Rome's bright hills,
  Or by the silvery Rhine,
You win all hearts to you, where'er
  Your glancing tresses shine;
But, darling, the love of the many,
  Is not a love like mine.

Last night I heard your voice in my dreams,
  I woke with a joyous thrill

To hear but the half-awakened birds,
   For the dark dawn lingered still,
And the lonesome sound of the waters,
   At the foot of Carey's hill.

Oh the pines are dark on Carey's hill,
   And the waters are black below.
But they shone like waves of jasper
   Upon one day I know,
The day I bore you out of the stream,
   With your face as white as snow.

You lay like a little lamb in my arms,
   So frail a thing, so weak,
And my coward lips said burning words
   They never had dared to speak
If they had not felt the chill of your brow,
   And the marble of your cheek.

Life had been but a bitter gift,
   That I fain would have thrown away,
But I could have thanked my God on my knees,
   For giving me life that day,
As I took you, lying so helpless,
   From the gates of death away.

How your noble kinsmen laughed and wept
   O'er their treasure snatched from the flood,

And your white-faced brother brought me gold—
   You loved him, or I could
Have obeyed the fiend that told me
   To curse him where he stood.

Gold! oh, darling, they had no need
   Such insults to repeat;
I knew the Heaven was above the earth,
   I knew, I knew, my sweet,
I was not worthy to touch the shoes
   That covered your dainty feet.

I knew as you laid your hand in mine,
   So kind as I turned away,
That we were severed as wide apart,
   That hour, as we are to-day,
And you in your stately English home,
   So far, so far away.

That soft white hand you laid in mine
   With a smile as I turned to go,
Oh, Lady Maud, I marvel
   If you ever stoop so low,
As to wonder what those tears meant,
   That glittered on its snow.

But I know if you had dreamed the truth
   Your beautiful dark brown eyes

Would only have grown more gentle,
   With a sorrowful surprise;
For a nobler and a kinder heart
   Ne'er beat beneath the skies.

You never meant to give me pain,
   But, oh, 'twas a cruel good,
I so low in the world's esteem,
   You of such noble blood,
That you stooped to as gentle words and deeds,
   As ever an angel could.

I blessed you for your brightness
   When you came unto our shore,
For the dull earth caught a beauty
   It never had before;
But you left a lonesome shadow,
   That will lie there evermore.

How proud the good ship bore you
   Adown the golden bay,
The sun's last light upon its sails—
   I stood there mournfully;
For I know it left the darkness—
   Took the sunlight all away.

THE HAUNTED CASTLE.

It stands alone on a haunted shore,
With curious words of deathless lore
   On its massive gate impearled;
And its carefully guarded mystic key
Locks in its silent mystery
   From the seeking eyes of the world.

Oft do its stately walls repeat
Echoes of music wildly sweet
   Swelling to gladness high—
With mournful ballads of ancient time,
And funeral hymns—and a nursery rhyme
   Dying away in a sigh.

Pictures out of each haunted room,
Up through the ghostly shadows loom,
   And gleam with a spectral light ;
Pictures lit with a radiant glow,
And some that image such desolate woe
   That, weeping, you turn from the sight.

Shining like stars in the twilight gloom
Brows as white as a lily's bloom

Gleam from its lattice and door;
And voices soft as a seraph's note,
Through its mysterious chambers float
  Back from eternity's shore.

In the mournful silence of midnight air
You hear on its stately and winding stair
  The echoes of fairy feet.
Gentle footsteps that lightly fall
Through the enchanted castle hall,
  And up in the golden street.

And still in a dark forsaken tower,
Crowned with a withered cypress flower,
  Is a bowed head turned away;
A face like carvéd marble white,
Sweet eyes drooping away from the light,
  Shunning the eye of day.

And oft when the light burns low and dim
A haggard form ungainly and grim
  Unbidden enters the door;
With chiding eyes whose burning light
You fain would bury in darkness and night,
  Never to meet you more.

Mysteries strange its still walls keep,
Strange are the forms that through it sweep—

Walking by night and by day.
But evermore will the castle hall
Echo their footsteps' phantom fall,
Till its walls shall crumble away.

THE STORY OF GLADYS.

"I LEAVE my child to Heaven." And with these words
Upon her lips, the Lady Mildred passed
Unto the rest prepared for her pure soul;
Words that meant only this: I cannot trust
Unto her earthly parent my young child,
So leave her to her heavenly Father's care;
And Heaven was gentle to the motherless,
And fair and sweet the maiden, Gladys, grew,
A pure white rose in the old castle set,
The while her father rioted abroad.

But as the day drew near when he should give,
By his dead lady's will, his child her own,
He having basely squandered all her wealth
To him intrusted, to his land returned,
And thrilled her trusting heart with terrors vague,
Of peril, of some shame to come to him,
Did she not yield unto his prayer—command,
That she would to Our Lady's convent go,
Forget the world and save him from disgrace.

But hidden as she had been all her life
From tender human ties, she loved the world

With all her loving heart, the fresh, free world
That God had made, and this life seemed to her
As but a living death.   A living tomb
The harsh stone walls that from the convent frowned
Upon the peaceful valley sweet with flowers.
The beautiful green valley, threaded by
Bright rivulets that sought the quiet lake,
Dear haunts sought daily by her maiden feet.
And " wilt thou not, for my sake ?" and " thou shalt
To save thy sire from shame !"   So wore the days,
And still she did not promise, though she wept
At his wild pleadings, trembled at his rage ;
Then of her mother's dying words he thought—
Her dying words—" I leave my child to Heaven."
And twisting them with his own wishes, wove
A chain therewith that bound her wavering will ;
A chain made mighty by the golden threads
Of rev'rence and of holy memories.
And so with heavy heart she gave her vow,
That in the autumn she would leave the world.
But first for one free summer did she pray.

And through those bright spring days she roamed abroad,
And poured upon the winds her low complaints ;
The while her dark soft eyes sought all the earth,
The beauteous earth that she too soon must leave ;
And all her mournful murmurs ended thus

With this sad cry of, " Oh, the happy world !"
Ended with these low words as with a sigh,
I will obey, but, "oh, the happy world !"

Oh, wondrous beauty of the morning skies !
   Oh, wide green fields with beady dew impearled !
The lark soars upward, singing as she flies,
   Oh, wave of free, swift wings, oh, happy world !

Oh, wordless wonder of the evening sky,
   Far ivory citadels with flags unfurled ;
Deep sapphire seas where rosy fleets float by
   The golden shores remote ; oh, happy world !

Oh, my blue violets by the laughing brook !
   My shy, sweet darlings, in your green leaves curled,
Bright eyes, sometime you will all vainly look
   For me, your lover.   Oh, the happy world !

So passed the days of spring, and she must sign
Dull papers to appease the hungry law,
And to the castle down a writer came ;
No graybeard old, and dryer than his tomes,
A tall, fair-faced youth, with bright, bold gaze,
And blood that leaped afresh like crimson wine,
Rash blood that led him to leap o'er a gate
Five-barred, within the mossy park, upon

The knight's old stumbling steed that played him false
To its own harm, for which it lost its life,
More fortunate the youth, though bruiséd he,
And bleeding from his many grievous wounds,
And Gladys tended him with gentlest care
Till love crept in and took the place of pain,
And in her heart took Pity's weeping place
And dwelt a king. He knew she was the bride
Of Heaven, not to be vexed with earthly love,
But yet, upon the last night of his stay,
As by the lake's low marge he met the maid,
And saw her soft eyes fall before his own,
He laid an almond blossom in her hand,
A blossom that both sweet and bitter is,
And said but this, " Say, is dear love a dream?"

" Nay, not a dream," she murmured, looking out
To where the light upon the waters lay,
A golden pathway leading to the sun,
"Dear love the wakening is, this life we live
Is but a dream." Then with a sudden hope
He would have caught her hands, but no, she clasped
Them o'er the snowy muslin on her breast,
And on her heart like drops of crimson blood,
There lay the almond blossoms, bitter, sweet ;
And far away her pure eyes looked adown
That shining path across the summer sea,

" Nay, life a long dream is, a sleep that lasts
Until we waken in the land of love."
But though thus calmly did she speak to him,
When he had gone to hide his breaking heart
As best he might, to bravely bide his time,
And do his life work as she bade him do,
Then all her lonely haunts echoed this cry,
This cry of deeper anguish—" Oh, my heart!"

Why did I pray for one more summer bright,
   The outward world but held me in time past;
Now, life and love have added links of might,
   A chain that fetters me, that holds me fast;
I will, I will obey, but oh, my heart!

My life was like some little mountain spring
   By slight waves stirred till some deep overflow
Swift breaks its peace, then with its risen king
   Down to the mighty deep it needs must go;
Thus did I follow love, but oh, my heart!

' For dear love sought me, claimed me for his own,
   And called me with his voice so strong, so low,
I followed unto bliss, thou hapless one,
   I did bethink me of my cruel vow,
The vow I will obey, but oh, my heart!

And through the long, still nights this cry was hers,
As on her couch she lay till dreary dawn,
Her large eyes dark with horror looking out
Upon the pitchy darkness unafraid.
And as the breathings of the new spring breeze,
Soft sighs of sad complaint, to autumn's storms
That hold the burdened sorrow of a year,
Was this, her sigh of, "oh, the happy world!"
To this despairing cry of, "oh, my heart!"
And as the year's late winds leave pale and chill
The earth, so did this weary cry of hers
So oft repeated leave her lips like snow.
And oft the lonely midnight heard her moan
Of hopes foregone, that women hold most dear.

" No little ones to ever cling to me
In closest love, look on me through his eyes
And call me mother, bless me with his smile."
Then low in tearful prayer her voice would sound
Despairing, wailing, through the lonely room,
The silent turret chamber steep and high,
" Thou maiden mother, Mary, knows my heart,
Thou who didst love and suffer, look on me,
Oh, pity me, sweet mother of the Christ !"

Then would the passion of her woe die out
In dreary calm, and as a chidden child

Who cries himself to rest, sobs in his sleep,
So pitifully would sound the latest words—
" I will, I will be patient, and obey."
But all the long days' silent anguish, all
These secret trysts she kept alone with pain
Wore her meek face, till like a spirit's looked
It, gleaming white from out her shadowy hair,
And so the last day came, the day of doom,
The dreaded day when she should leave the world.

But He who holdeth little useless birds
In His protecting care, looked tenderly
Upon this patient soul, so sorely tried.
This sweet soul purified by all its pain,
For on this day, so fair a morn, it seemed
A heavenly peace sunk down to this sad earth
From gate ajar, the bright and pearly gate
Swung widely open for an angel guest.
A faithful servant climbed the winding stair,
Sent by her eager father with the dawn
To rouse her, tell her that the hour had come
When she to save his name should leave the world.
And as the woman stood beside the couch
She said, " Sweet soul, she talks out in her sleep."
For there she lay with closed eyes murmuring low,
With mournful brow and sad lips, " oh, dear love."
Then cried out with a sob, " 'tis not a dream."

Then spake of blood-red blossoms, bitter, sweet,
And with her white lips sighing this, she sunk
Into what seemed to be a dreamless sleep.

And as the loving servant weeping stood,
Loath to awake her to her evil doom,
She opened her large violet eyes, and gazed
Upon the morning sunlight stealing in ;
The clear light trembling, growing on the wall,
And as she looked, her eyes grew like the eyes
Of blessed angels looking on their Lord.
And high toward Heaven she lifted up her hands,
Then clasped them in content upon her breast.
And cried out in a glad voice, " oh, my heart !"
And with such glory lighting up her face,
As if the flood of joy had filled her heart,
And overrun her lips with blissful smiles,
She left the world, and saved her sire from shame.

FAREWELL.

Lift up your brown eyes, darling,
  Not timidly and shy,
As in the fair, lost past, not thus
  I'd have you meet my eye.
But grave, and calm, and earnest,
  Thus bravely should we part,
Not sorrowfully, not lightly,
  And so farewell, dear heart.

Yes, fare thee well, farewell,
  Whate'er shall me betide
May gentlest angels comfort thee,
  And peace with thee abide ;
Our love was but a stormy love,
  'Tis your will we should part—
So smile upon me once, darling,
  And then farewell, dear heart.

But lay your hand once on my brow,
  Set like a saintly crown,
It will shield me, it will help me
  To hurl temptations down.

God give thee better love than mine—
Nay, dear, no tears must start,
See, I am quiet, thou must be,
And now farewell, dear heart.

THE KNIGHT OF NORMANDY.

CLEAR shone the moon, my mansion walls
  Towered white above the wood.
Near, down the dark oak avenue
  An humble cottage stood.

My gardener's cottage, small and brown,
  Yet precious unto me;
For there she dwelt, who sat by me
  That night beside the sea.

So sweet, the white rose on her neck
  Was not more fair than she,
As silently her soft brown eyes
  Looked outward o'er the sea.

So still, the muslin o'er her heart
  Seemed with no breath to stir,
As silently she sat and heard
  The tale I told to her.

"It was a knight of Normandy.
  He vowed on his good sword
He would not wed his father's choice,
  The Lady Hildegarde.

" Near dwelt the beauteous Edith.
    A lowly maiden she—"
Ah ! still unmoved, her dark sweet eyes
    Looked far away from me.

" Dearer to him one blossom small
    That had but touched her hand,
Than all the high-born beauties—
    The ladies of the land.

" Dearer to him," quick came my breath
    As I looked down on her,
But the white roses in her hand
    No lightest leaf did stir.

Ah ! wistfully I read her face,
    Full gently did I speak,
No light dawned in her tender eye,
    No flush stole o'er her cheek.

" He wore her colors on the field.
    He went where brave hearts were ;
Ah, gallantly and nobly
    He fought for love of her.

" He loved her with his whole true heart,"
    Now like a sudden flame
Up to her cheek so pure and white,
    A flood of crimson came.

Her hands unclasped, down to her feet
  My flowers unnoticed shook;
I leaned and followed with my gaze
  Her glad and eager look.

I saw a boat sweep round the rock,
  Rowed with a steady grace;
I saw the fisher's manly form,
  His brown and handsome face.

" For love of her, to victory
  He his brave squadron led,
Then broke his true heart, and her scarf
  Pillowed his dying head.

" So died this knight of Normandy,
  Died with his sword unstained;"
I know not that she heard my words,
  So near the boat had gained.

I said, Heaven bless her, in my heart,
  She had no thought for me;
I turned away and left them there
  Beside the beating sea.

Behind me lay the sweet moonlight,
  My shadow went before,
And passed a dark and gloomy shape
  Before me through the door.

O strange and sad this life of ours,
   This life beneath the sun ;
O sad and strange and full of pain
   God help us, every one.

God help us, that we may endure
   Like him of Normandy ;
And die with sword unstained, that has
   Led us to victory.

SOMETIME.

On the shore I sit and gaze
    Out on the twilight sea,
For my ship may come, though many days
    I have waited patiently;
With waiting trusting eyes,
    A lonely watch I keep
For its silver sails to rise
    Like a blossom out of the deep.

It is built of a costly wood,
    Bearing the strange perfume
Of the gorgeous solitude,
    Where it grew in tropical gloom:
And the odorous scent, the spicy balm
    Of its isle it will bear to me,
As I stand on the shore, in the magic calm,
    And my ship comes in from sea.

It is laden with all that is sweet
    Of the beauty of every clime;
Slowly and proudly 'twill glide to my feet
    In the eve of that fair " Sometime,"

Before me its sails will be furled,
    A princess I shall be,
Crowned with the wealth of the world,
    When my ship comes in from sea.

Sweet faces I then shall see,
    Tender, undoubting, true,
Soft hands will be stretched to me
    With a welcome I never knew ;
In the peace of such tenderness
    I shall rest forevermore,
And weep in my perfect bliss,
    As I never wept before.

Sometimes I think it is not far
    And I bend my head and list,
For I think I see a slender spar
    Gleam through the golden mist ;
And I fancy I hear the sound
    Of wind in a silken sail,
And an odor rare from Eastern ground,
    Floats in on the languid gale.

But I sit and watch the west
    Till the sun goes down, in vain ;
It was only a cloud with an ivory crest,
    A cloud of vapor and rain ;

It rises and hides the sea,
   And my heart grows chill and numb,
Lest this terrible thing should be,
   That my ship will never come.

But the morn is bright—the wave
   Is a golden and shining track,
Softly the waters the white sands lave,
   And my trusting faith comes back ;
Oh, all that I ever lost,
   And all that I long to be,
Will be mine when the deep is crossed,
   And my ship comes home from sea.

MOTIVES.

I SAID that I would see
   Her once, to curse her fair, deceitful grace,
To curse her for my life-long agony;
   But when I saw her face,
I said, "Sweet Christ, forgive both her and me."

High swelled the chanted hymn,
   Low on the marble swept the velvet pall.
I bent above her, and my eyes grew dim,
   My sad heart saw it all—
She loved me, loved me though she wedded him.

And then shot through my soul
   A thrill of fierce delight, to think that he
Must yield her form, his all, to Death's control,
   The while her love for me
Would live, when sun and stars had ceased to roll.

But no, on the white brow,
   Graved in its marble, was deep calm impressed,
Saying that peace had come to her through woe;
   Saying, she had found rest
At last, and I, I must not love her now.

It may be in Heaven's grace,
　Beneath the shade of some immortal palm,
That God will let me see her angel face ;
　Then wild, wild heart be calm,
Wipe out that old love, every sorrowful trace.

I know that if it be,
　We two should meet again in Paradise.
'Twould trouble her pure soul if she should see
　The old grief in my eyes ;
'Twould grieve her dear heart through eternity.

Wipe out that grief, my soul,
　And shall I lose all love, in losing this ?
Unclasp my spirit, self's close stolid stole.
　Are there no lives to bless ?
So will I give my love, my life, no stinted dole.

God will note deeds and sighs,
　Throned in far splendor on the heavenly hill,
Though mad sounds from this wretched planet rise—
　Moans wild enough to fill
Heaven's air, and drown its harps in doleful cries.

And angels shall look down,
　Through incense rising from my godly deeds.
Approving gleam those eyes of tender brown ;
　Sure on a brow that bleeds,
The thorns should change to a more glorious crown.

Well done, my soul, well done,
  Out of thy grief to rear a ladder tall
To reach the land that lies beyond the sun,
  To scale the jasper wall,
And rise to glory on grief's stepping-stone.

God looks into the tide,
  Angel and demon troubled, of a man's mind :
And if my alms are scattered far and wide,
  Only my love to find,
Only to pave a path to reach her side—

Will He accept from me
  My worship, gifts—the heavens are very still,
No answer do I hear, no sign I see,
  If I but knew His will ;
Would He would come a-walking on the sea.

————

The storm is overpast, for sweet and fair
  A sudden radiance shone o'er wave and lea :
And in the glory trembling through the air,
  He came unto me walking on the sea.

The heavy waves that had rushed to and fro
  Cowered at His feet in sudden melody ;
And all transfigured in the shining glow
  Did He come to me walking on the sea.

Far off I saw His form, but knew it not ;
   He nearer drew, He smiled, my fears did flee ;
His loving look dispelled a lingering doubt,
   As He came to me o'er the twilight sea.

I dropped my burden on the shelving sand
   So I might meet Him, if such bliss could be,
I reached the shore, I knelt and kissed His hand
   With blissful tears beside the twilight sea.

Such love He woke, I would my life have lain
   Low down to pave His way, " He loveth me
Who loveth this sad world, and blesseth man,"
   Came blown to me across the twilight sea.

Perplexing questions died within my breast,
   " Deep peace hath he who doeth lovingly
My will, who loveth most, he loveth best,"
   Came blown to me across the twilight sea.

The storm was overpast, a breath of balm
   Lapped the low waves, and lingered on the lea,
For in the twilight fell a holy calm,
   He came unto me walking on the sea.

Was this a dream?   If it were not a dream
   My life is blest in truth, and if it be,
I know across the deep has fallen a gleam,
   A bridge of glory spans the twilight sea.

NIGHTFALL.

Soft o'er the meadow, and murmuring mere,
Falleth a shadow, near and more near ;
Day like a white dove floats down the sky,
Cometh the night, love, darkness is nigh ;
    So dies the happiest day.

Slow in thy dark eye riseth a tear,
Hear I thy sad sigh, Sorrow is near :
Hope smiling bright, love, dies on my breast,
As day like a white dove flies down the west ;
    So dies the happiest day.

HIS PLACE.

So all things come to our mind at last,
  He is close by your side in the twilight gloom,
  And you two are alone in the dim old room,
Yet he is mute, as you bade him be, time past.

You bade him to weary you, never again
  With his idle love, in truth he was wise,
  For he spake no more, although in his eyes
You read, you fancied, a language of pain.

But this is past, and vex you he never will,
  With loving glance, or look of sad reproach ;
  His lips move not, smile not at your approach :
The flowers he clasps are not more calm and still.

Your favorite flowers he has heard you praise,
  Purple pansies, and lilies creamy white ;
  But he offers them not to you to-night,
He troubles you not, he has learned " his place."

You wished to teach him that lesson, you told
  Him as much, you know, in this very room,
  'Twas about this hour, for the twilight gloom
As now, was enwrapping you, fold on fold.

Was "his place" in the haunts of the herded poor,
  Where the pestilence stalked with deadly breath?
  Face to face with its dreadful shadow, death,
How he wrestled with it from door to door,

Giving his life that others life might find,
  Shaming you with his toil, his bravery,
  Not by a word or look, no boaster he,
He was always gentle to you, and kind.

He has found "his place," but no need of fears,
  No; you need not summon your jealous pride,
  For "his place" will never be by your side,
Nevermore, nevermore, through all the years.

And when from Time shall drop Earth's days
  Like chaff from the bloom of the year sublime,
  With the gentle spirits of every time,
And the martyr souls, he will find his place.

So answers will come to our seeking wills,
  Nevermore will his sad face vex your sight,
  For you never will make your robes so white
As to stand by him on the heavenly hills.

Yes, lay your cheek upon his, and press
  The clustering hair from his broad white brow,
  Have no fear, he will not annoy you now
By a word in praise of your loveliness.

Yes, kneel by him, moaning, kissing his brow,
　　Not now will it grieve him, your tears' swift rain,
　　And he will not ask you to share your pain;
Ah! Once he would, but not now—not now.

So leave the old room in the waning light,
　　Go out in your peerless beauty and pride,
　　And let no shadow go out by your side
To follow you under the falling night.

A DREAM OF SPRING.

The world is asleep! All hushed is Nature's warm, sweet
    breath.
  The world is asleep, and dreaming the silent dream of
    snow,
But through the silence that seems like the silence of death,
  Under their shroud of ermine, the souls of the roses glow.

And forever the heart of the water throbs and beats,
  Though bound by a million gleaming fetters and crystal
    rings,
No sound on lonesome mornings the lonely watcher greets,
  But the frosty pane is impressed with the shadow of com-
    ing wings.

WAITING.

I KNOW not where you wait for me in all your maiden
    sweetness,
Sweet soul in whom my life will find its rest, its full com-
    pleteness ;
But somewhere you await me, Fate will lead us to each
    other,
As roses know the sunlight, so shall we know one an-
    other.

Dear heart, what are you doing in this twilight's purple
    splendor,
Do you tend your dewy flowers with fingers white and
    slender,
Heavy, odor-laden branches in blessing bent above you,
Fond lilies kneeling at your feet, winds murmuring they
    love you?

Mayhap, your heart in maiden peace is like a closed bud
    sleeping,
Wrapped in pure folds of saintly thought, its tender fresh-
    ness keeping.

Yet like a dream that comes in sleep, your soul   sweet quiet
      breaking,
Is a thought of me, my darling, that shall come true on
      waking.

Perchance you turn from passionate vows, words wild with
      love's sweet madness,
With soft eyes looking far away, in yearning trust and sad-
      ness ;
A look that tells his alien soul how widely you are parted,
Though he knows not whom your rapt eyes seek, my sweet,
      my loving-hearted.

Oh, the world is rough ; the heart against its sneers, its cold
      derision,
Locks all its better feelings, making it a gloomy prison ;
But your hand, my angel, shall unlock its rocky, dust-strewn
      portal,
Your smile shall rouse its dying dreams of good to life im-
      mortal.

You will make me better, purer, for love, the true refiner,
Burning out the baser passions, will kindle the diviner,
Will plead and win my spirit, not to shame its heavenly
      station,
You will trust me, and that trust will prove my tempted
      soul's salvation.

God keep you tenderly, my life's dear hope and unseen
blessing;
Oh, night wind, touch her tresses till I come with fond
caressing,
Thy crown of pearl-linked light, oh, royal moon stoop down
and give her,
Till queen of love's own kingdom, I crown her mine forever.

A SONG FOR TWILIGHT.

On! the day was dark and dreary,
　For clouds swept o'er the sun,
The burden of life seemed heavy,
　And its warfare never done;
But I heard a voice at twilight,
　It whispered in my ear.
" Oh, doubting heart, look upward,
　Dear soul, be of good cheer.
Oh, weary heart, look upward,
　Dear soul, be of good cheer."

And lo! on looking upward
　The stars lit up the sky
Like the lights of an endless city,
　A city set on high.
And my heart forgot its sorrow
　These heavenly homes to see—
Sure in those many mansions
　Is room for even me,
Sure in those many mansions,
　Is room for thee and me.

THE FLIGHT.

HERE in the silent doorway let me linger
    One moment, for the porch is still and lonely ;
That shadow's but the rose vine in the moonlight ;
    All are asleep in peace, I waken only,
And he I wait, by my own heart's beating
    I know how slow to him the tide creeps by,
Nor life, nor death, could bar our hearts from meeting :
    Were worlds between, his soul to mine would fly.

Oh, shame ! to think a heap of paltry metal
    Should overbalance manhood's noblest graces ;
A film of gold had gilt his worth and honor,
    Warming to smiles the coldness of their faces ;
Gentle to me, they rise in condemnation,
    And plead with me than words more powerfully.
Oh ! well I love them—but they have wealth and station
    To fill their hearts, and he has only me.

But oh, my roses, how their great pure faces
    Beseech me as they bend from sculptured column.
So with my wet cheek closely pressed against them,
    I listen to their pleadings sweet and solemn.

Oh, Memory, if an hour of gloom and grieving
　I here have known, that hour before me set;
But all the peace and joy I am leaving,
　In mercy, Memory, let me forget.

Oh, home! if here a frown has ever chilled me,
　Let it now rise and darken on my sight.
If a harsh word or look has ever grieved me,
　Let me remember that harsh word to-night.
But all the tender words, the fond caressing,
　The loving smiles that daily I have met,
The patient mother love, God's crowning blessing,
　In mercy, Memory, let me forget.

Here she has kissed me with fond looks of greeting;
　Will that smile fade when waiting me no longer?
Oh, true first love, tender and changing never;
　But there's a love that nearer is and stronger—
He comes! I kneel and kiss the stone, oh, mother,
　Where you have stood and blessed me with your eyes;
Forgive—forgive me, mother—father—brother—
　For oh, he loves me—and love sanctifies.

COMFORT.

Once through an autumn wood
 · I roamed in tearful mood,
By grief dismayed, doubting, and ill at ease;
 When from a leafless oak,
 Methought low murmurs broke,
Complaining accents, as of words like these:

 " Incline thy mighty ear
 Great Mother Earth, and hear
How I, thy child, am sorely vexed and tossed;
 No one to heed my moan,   ·
 I shudder here, alone
With my destroyers, wind and snow, and frost.

 Then low and unaware
 This answer cleaved the air,
This tender answer, " Doubting one be still;
 Oh trust to me, and know
 The wind, the frost, the snow,
Are but my servants sent to do my will.

 " For the destroyer frost,
 His labor is not lost,

Rid thee he shall of many noisome things ;
   And thou shalt praise the snow
   When drinking far below
Refreshment sweet from overflowing springs.

   " My child thou'rt not alone,
   I love thee, hear thy moan,
But winds that fret thee only causeth thee
   To more securely stand,
   More firmly clasp my hand,
And soaring upward, closer cling to me."

   Then from my burdened heart
   The shadows did depart,
Then said I softly—" winds of sorrow blow
   So I but closer cling
   To thee, my Lord, my King,
Who loves me, even me, so weak and low."

JENNY ALLEN.

I NEVER shall hear your voice again,
  Your voice so gentle and low ;
But the thought of you, Jenny Allen,
  Will go with me where I go.
Your sweet voice drowns the Atlantic wave
  And the rush of the Alpine snow.

You were very fair, Jenny Allen,
  Fair as a woodland rose ;
Your heart was pure as an angel's heart,
  Too good for earth and its woes,
And I loved you, Jenny Allen,
  With a sorrowful love, God knows.

You loved me, Jenny Allen,
  My sorrow made me wise ;
And I read your heart, 'twas an easy task,
  For within your clear blue eyes,
Your pure and innocent thoughts shone out
  Like stars from the summer skies.

He had riches and fame with his seventy years
  When he won you for his wife ;

You were but a child, and poor, and tired,
   Tired of toil and strife ;
And you only thought of rest, poor dove,
   When you sold your beautiful life.

Alas, for the hour I entered in
   Your halls of lordly mirth ;
For I lost there, Jenny Allen,
   All that gives life worth ;
You taught your teacher, Jenny,
   The saddest lesson of earth.

Ah, woe's the hour I ever stepped
   Your mansion walls within ;
For you loved me, Jenny Allen,
   But you never dreamed 'twas sin ;
Your heart was white as a lily's heart,
   When it drinks the sunshine in.

God pity me, Jenny Allen,
   That I ever loved you so,
I would have died to give you peace,
   And I only gave you woe ;
For your eyes looked like a wounded dove's,
   When I told you I must go.

You were but a child, Jenny Allen,
   But that hour made you wise ;

A woman's grief and holy strength
　Sprang up in your mournful eyes;
Ah, you were an angel, Jenny,
　An angel in woman's guise.

But a pitiful, pitiful look, Jenny,
　Your seraph features wore,
As I left you that dark autumn morn,
　Left you forevermore;
And heaven seemed shut against me
　As I blindly shut that door.

The years have rained on you golden gifts,
　You dwell in a queenly show;
There are jewels of price in your silken hair,
　And upon your neck of snow.
Do you ever think of me, Jenny,
　And the dream of the long ago!

I have sat me down under foreign skies
　Afire with an Orient glow;
I have seen the moon gild the desert sand,
　And silver the Arctic snow,
But the thought of you, Jenny Allen,
　Goes with me where I go.

THE UNSEEN CITY.

Not far away does that bright city stand,
  'Tis but the mist o'er its dividing stream,
That wraps the glory of its glitt'ring strand,
  Its radiant skies, and mountains silvery gleam;
Oh, often in the blindness of our fate
We wander very near the city's gate.

We love that unseen city, and we yearn
  Ever within our earthly homes to see
Its golden towers, that in the sunset burn,
  Its white walls rising from the quiet sea;
Its mansions gleaming with immortal glow,
Filled with the treasure lost to us below.

Yes, dear ones that we loved and lost are there;
  Bright in that fair clime beam those sweet eyes now;
Fanned by its soft breeze floats the shining hair,
  Hair we have smoothed back from the gentlest brow;
Softest white hands we kissed and clasped in ours
Slipped from our grasp, lured by its glowing flowers.

Fairer it seems, its velvet walks were sweet,
  Dearer its quiet streets, with gold paved o'er,

Since o'er them lightly fall the little feet—
　The light feet bounding through our homes no more;
Oh, heart's dear music, tearfully missed,
That city's filled with melody like this.

It is not far away; down from its arches roll
　Anthems too sacred for the outward ear,
Pouring their haunting sweetness on the soul;
　Oh, how our waiting spirits thrill to hear,
In listening to the low bewildering strain,
Voices they said we should not hear again.

Oh, dear to us that city.　He is there,
　He whom unseen we love; no need of light;
His tender eyes illume the crystal air
　Where His belovéd walk in vesture white,
What though on earth they wandered, poor, distressed,
And saw through tears His glory, now they rest.

Oh, that fair city, shining o'er the tide,
　Thither we journey through the storm and night;
But soon shall we adown its still bay glide,
　Soon will the city's gate gleam on our sight,
There with our own forever shall we be,
In that fair city rising from the sea.

THE WAGES OF SIN.

I AM an outcast, sinful and vile I know,
  But what are you, my lady, so fair, and proud, and high?
The fringe of your robe just touched me, me so low—
  Your feet defiled, I saw the scorn in your eye,
And the jeweled hand, that drew back your garments fine.
  What should you say if I told you to your face
Your robes are dyed with as deep a stain as mine,
  The only difference is you are better paid for disgrace.

You loved a man, you promised to be his bride,
  Strong vows you gave, you were in the sight of Heaven
        his wife,
And when you sold yourself for another's wealth, he died;
  And what is that but murder? To take a life
That is a little beyond my guilt, I ween,
  To murder the one you love is a crime of deeper grade
Than mine, yet in purple you walk on the earth a queen;
  I think the wages of sin are very unequally paid.

For what did you receive when you sold yourself for his gold,
  When with guilty loathing you plighted your white, false
        hand,

A palace in town and country, his name long centuries old,
  A carriage with coachmen and footmen, wealth in broad
    tracts of land,
Wealth in coffers and vaults, high station, the family gems,
  For these you stood at God's altar and swore to a lie;
But smother your conscience to silence if it condemns,
  With this you are liberally paid for your life of infamy.

What wages did I receive when I gave myself for his love,
  So young, so weak, and loving him, loving him so—-
What did I get for my sin, O merciful God above!
  But the terrible, terrible wages—pain and want and woe;
The world's scorn, and my own contempt and disdain,
  The hideous hue of guilt that stares in every eye.
Like you I cannot 'broider with gold my garments' stain,
  You see, my lady, you get far better wages than I.

In your constancy to sin you far exceed my power,
  Since that day marked with blackness from other days—
The day before your marriage—never since that hour
  Have I heard his voice, have I looked upon his face;
For I threw his gold at his feet and stole away
  Anywhere—anywhere—only out of his sight,
Longing to hide from the mocking glare of the day,
  Longing to cover my eyes forever away from the light.

And long I strove to hate him, for I thought
  I was so young, a friendless orphan left to his care.

It was a terrible sin that he had wrought,
  And since I had the burden of guilt to bear
It was enough without the wild despair of love,
  So I strove to reason my passionate love to hate.
Can we kneel with tears and bid the strong sun move
  Away from the sky?   It is vain to war with fate.

That a hard life I have lived since then, 'tis true,
  My hands are unblackened by sinful wages since that day,
And my baby died, I was not fit, God knew
  To guide a sinless soul, so He took my bird away;
And my heart was empty and lone as a robin's winter nest,
  Without the trusting eyes that never looked scornfully,
The head that nestled fearlessly on my guilty breast,
  And the little constant hands that clung to me, even me.

But I knew it were best for God to unclasp her hand
  From mine, while yet she clung to it in trust,
Than for her to draw it from me, live to understand,
  Blush for her mother—had she lived she must.
And then she had her father's smile, and his soft, dark eyes,
  Maybe she would have had his fair, false ways—his heart.
It is well that she passed through the starry gate of the skies
  Though it closed and bars us forever and ever apart.

For I am a sinful woman, well I know,
  And though by others' sins my own are not excused,

Things seem so strange to me in this strange world of woe,
  In a maze of doubt and wonder I get confused ;
Whether a sin of impulse, born of a fatal love,
  Is worse than deliberate bargain, a life of legal shame,
Legal below, I think in the courts above
  The heavenly scribes will call a crime by its right name.

But we stand before the wise, wise judgment-seat
  Of the world, and it calls you pure,
That in your pearl-gemmed breast all saintly virtues meet,
  Holier than other holy women, higher, truer,
So sweet a creature, an angel in woman's guise.
    They would not wonder much, though much they might
        admire,
Should you be caught again up to your native skies
  From an alien world in a chariot of fire.

So we stand before the tender judgment-seat
  Of the world, and it calls me vile,
So low that it is a wonder God will let
  His joyous sunshine gild my guilty head with its smiles.
An outcast barred beyond the pale of hope,
  Beyond the lamp of their mercy's flickering light.
They would scarcely wonder if the earth should ope
  And swallow up the wretch from their vexed sight.

Before another judgment-seat one day we will stand
  You and I, my lady, and he by our side.

He who won my heart, who held my life in his hand,
  He who bought you with gold to be his bride;
Before an assembled world we shall stand, we three,
    To meet from the merciful Judge our doom of weal or
      woe,
He holds His righteous balance true and evenly,
  And which is the vilest sinner we then shall know.

ISABELLE AND I.

ISABELLE has gold, and lands,
  Fate gave her a fair lot;
Like the white lilies of the field
  Her soft hands toil not.
I gaze upon her splendor
  Without an envious sigh;
I have no wealth in lands and gold,
  And yet sweet peace have I.

I know the blue sky smiles as bright
  On the low field violet,
As on the proud crest of the pine
  On loftiest mountain set.
I am content—God loveth all,
  And if He tenderly
The sparrow guides, He knoweth best
  The place where I should be.

Her violet velvet curtains trail
  Down to the marble floor,
But brightly God's rich sunshine streams
  Into my cottage door;

And not a picture on her walls,
   Hath beauty unto me,
Like that which from my window frame
   I daily lean to see.

She has known such pomp, she careth not
   For any humble sight;
Flowers bending o'er the brook's green edge,
   To her give no delight;
She tends her costly-eastern bird
   With gold upon its wing;
But her wild roses bloom for me,
   For me her wild birds sing.

She tires of home, and fain would see
   The brightest climes of earth,
And so she sails for summer lands
   With friends to share her mirth;
She waves her jewelled hand to me
   The opal spray-clouds fly;
She leaves me with the fading shore—
   Do I envy her? not I.

She will see the sailors' hardened palms
   Curbing the toiling sails,
She will faint beneath the tropic calms
   And face the angry gales.

She will labor for her happiness
   While I've no need to speak,
But on a lotus leaf I float,
   Unto the land they seek.

There, like a dream from out the wave,
   I see a city rise,
I stand entranced, as by a spell,
   Upon the Bridge of Sighs.
The low and measured dip of oars
   Falls softly on my ear
Blent with the tender evening song,
   Of some swart gondolier.

And down from marble terraces
   Veiled ladies slowly pass,
And, entering antique barges,
   Glide down the streets of glass ;
And eyes filled with the dew and fire
   Of their own midnight sky,
Gleam full on me, as silently
   The gondolas float by.

The sunset burns, and turns the wave
   To an enchanted stream,
And far up on the shadowy steeps
   The white walled convents gleam,

The music of their bells float out—
  The sweet wind bears it by,
Adown the warm and sunny slopes,
  Where purple vineyards lie.

And I stand in old cathedrals,
  By tombs of buried kings,
White angels bend above them—
  Mute guard with folded wings.
Far down the aisle the organ peals,
  The priests are knelt in prayer
And memories flood its ancient walls,
  As the music fills the air.

I may not see that blessed land,
  But she roams o'er the sod
The Lord's pure eyes have hallowéd,
  Where once His feet have trod.
Yet He in mercy has drawn near,
  He has me comforted—
So near He seemed I almost felt
  His hand upon my head.

And I with slow and reverent steps
  Through ancient cities roam,
Treading o'er crumbling columns,
  The dust of spire and dome;

The tall and shattered arches
　Their flickering shadows cast,
Like bent and hoary spectres,
　Low murmuring of the past.

And Isabelle toils o'er the Alps,
　Through fields of ice and snow,
To see the lofty glaciers
　Flash in the sun's red glow.
I feel no cold, and yet on high
　Their shining spires I see.
Why should I envy Isabelle?
　Why should she pity me?

Why should I envy Isabelle
　When thus so easily,
Upon a tropic flower's perfume
　I float across the sea?

GOOD-BY.

Again I see that May moon shine,
Dost thou remember, soul of mine?
I held your hand in mine, you know,
And as I bent to whisper low,
A tender light was in your eye,
" Sweetheart, good-by, sweetheart, good-by."

There came a time my lips were white
Beneath the pale and cold moonlight,
And burning words I might not speak,
You read, love, in my ashen cheek,
As my whole heart breathed in this one cry,
" Sweetheart, good-by, sweetheart, good-by."

Time's waves that roll so swift and fleet
Have borne you far from me, my sweet,
Have borne you to a sunny bay,
Where brightest sunshine gilds your way,
Do these words ever dim your sky—
Sweetheart, good-by, sweetheart, good-by!

I cannot tell, but this I know
They go with me where'er I go,

I hear them in the crowded mart,
At midnight lone, they chill my heart—
They dim for me the earth and sky,
Sweetheart, good-by, sweetheart, good-by.

And in that hour of mystery,
When loved ones shall bend over me,
Near ones to kiss my lips and weep,
As nearer steals the dreamless sleep,
From all I'll turn with this last sigh,
" Sweetheart, good-by, sweetheart, good-by."

THE SEA-CAPTAIN'S WOOING.

Put the crown of your love on my forehead,
   Its sweet links clasped with a kiss,
And all the great monarchs of England
   Never wore such a gem as this.
Give me your hand, little maiden,
   That sceptre so pearly white,
And I'll envy not the kingliest wand
   That ever waved in might.

I know 'tis like asking a morning cloud
   With a grim old mountain to stay,
But your love would soften its ruggedness,
   And melt its roughness away.
I have seen a delicate rosy cloud,
   A rough, gray cliff enfold,
Till his heart was warmed by its loveliness,
   And his brow was tinged with its gold.

Oh, poor and mean does my life show
   Compared with the beauty of thine,
Like a diamond embedded in granite
   Your life would be set in mine :

But a faithful love should guard you,
　And shelter you from life's storm,
The rock must be shivered to atoms
　Ere its treasure should come to harm.

How your sweet face has shone on me
　From the tropics' midnight sea,
When the sailors slept, and I kept watch
　Alone with my God and thee.
I know your heart is relenting,
　The tender look in your eyes
Seems like that sky's soft splendor
　When the sun was beginning to rise.

You need not veil their glorious light
　With your eyelids' cloud of snow,
A tell-tale bird with a crimson wing
　On your cheek flies to and fro;
And whispers to me such blissful hope
　That my foolish tears will start,
Ah, little bird! your fluttering wing
　Is folded on my heart.

IONE.

I MIGHT strive as well to melt to softness the soulless breast
  Of some fair and saintly image, carven out of stone,
With my smile, as to stir your heart from its icy rest,
  Or win a tender glance from your royal eyes, Ione;
But your sad smile lures me on, as toward some fatal rock
  Is the fond wave drawn, but to break with passionate
    moan.
Break! to be spurned from its cold feet with a stony shock,
  As you would spurn my suppliant heart from your feet,
    Ione.

Ione, there is a grave in the churchyard under the hill,
  The villagers shun like the unblest haunt of a ghost,
Dropped there out of a dark spring night, I remember still,
  For a foreign ship had anchored that night on the coast:
On the gray stone tablet is written this one word "Rest."
  Did he who sleeps underneath seek for it vainly here?
What is the secret hidden there in the buried breast,
  The secret deeper sunken by dripping rains each year.

When autumn's bending boughs and harvests burdened the
    ground
  An early laborer, chancing to pass that way alone,

Saw a small glove gleaming whitely upon the mound,
 And into the delicate wrist was woven " Ione,"
And he said as he dropped it again his eye did mark—
 For this unknown, unhallowed grave had been shunned by
  all—
A narrow footpath winding through to the lofty wall,
 That guards the wild grandeur and gloom of your fa-
  ther's park.

'Tis well to put small faith in a simple rustic's eye,
 This story your father heard, and haughtily denied,
The grass waves rankly now, and gives the fellow the lie,
 How many secrets the tall, deceitful grasses hide,
Patting the turf that covers a maiden's innocent rest,
 And creeping and winding old haunted ruins among,
As silently smooth's the mould above the murdered breast,
 Smothering down to deeper silence a buried wrong.

In your father's gallery once, I saw your pictured face,
 Ione you were not always so sad and pale as this,
No beauty in all the long line of your noble race
 Had eyes so softly bathed in bright bewitchment of
  bliss,
You were just nineteen, they said—it was painted in Spain
 The year before you came—it was on your foreign tour,
By an artist too low to be reached by your disdain,
 A delicate, passionate-hearted boy, proud and poor.

So said the rumors floating to us across the sea,
  You had only an invalid mother with you there,
I fancy that then you set your heart's pure feelings free
  For the first time, far from your proud old father's care,
For you used to wander down the shaded garden ways,
  Your slight hand closely clasped by the fair-haired English
    youth,
His blue eyes bent on your blushing face, so rumor says,
  Though such light birds are not to be trusted much in
    truth.

Your face is not the face that looked from the antique frame,
  Ione, and even that is gone from the oaken wall;
That picture that never was painted for gold or fame,
  So vowed the artist friend who went with me to the hall;
But the pain on your white brow sits regally I ween,
  The smile on your perfect lips is perilously sweet,
My slavish glances crown you my love, my fate, my queen,
  As you pass in peerless beauty adown the village street.

SUMMER DAYS.

LIKE emerald lakes the meadows lie,
   And daisies dot the main ;
The sunbeams from the deep blue sky
   Drop down in golden rain,
And gild the lily's silver bell,
   And coax buds apart,
But I miss the sunshine of my youth,
   The summer of my heart.

The wild birds sing the same glad song
   They sang in days of yore ;
The laughing rivulet glides along,
   Low whispering to the shore,
And its mystic water turns to gold
   The sunbeam's quivering dart,
But I miss the sunshine of my youth,
   The summer of my heart.

The south wind murmurs tenderly
   To the complaining leaves ;
The Flower Queen gorgeous tapestry
   Of rose and purple weaves.

Yes, Nature's smile, the weary while,
　Wears all its olden truth,
But I miss the sunshine of my heart,
　The summer of my youth.

THE LADY CECILE.

Sitting alone in the windy tower,
  While the waves leap high, or are low at rest,
What does she think of, hour by hour,
  With her strange eyes bent on the distant west,
  And a fresh white rose on her withered breast,
What does she think of, hour by hour?
                          The Lady Cecile.

Low under the lattice, day by day,
  White homeward sails like swallows come,
But the sad eyes look afar and away,
  And the sailors' songs as they near their home.
  No glance may win, for she sitteth dumb,
With her sad eyes looking afar and away,
                          The Lady Cecile.

Just forty years has she dwelt alone
  With an ancient servant, grim and gray,
Sat alone under sun and moon ;
  But once each year, on the third of June,
  She treads the creaking staircase down,
But back in her tower with the dying day,
                          Is the Lady Cecile.

Beneath the tower of the lonesome hall,
  Stone stairs creep down where the slow tide flows,
There, out of a niche in the mouldering wall,
  Low leaneth a royal tropical rose :
    Who set it there none cares, nor knows.
Long years ago in the mouldering wall,
               But the Lady Cecile.

But each third of June as the sun dips low,
  She descends the stairs to the water's verge.
And plucks a rose from the lowest bough
  Which the lapping waves almost submerge.
    And what forms out of the deep, resurge
To vex her, maybe, with mournful brow,
              Knows the Lady Cecile.

Her locks are sown with silver hairs,
  And the face they shroud is pale and wan :
Once it was sweet as the rose she wears,
  Though the perfect lips wore a proud disdain !
    But the rose-face paled by time and pain,
No new springs know, like the flower she wears,
              The Lady Cecile.

Why does she set the fresh white rose
  So faithfully over her silent breast ?
And what her thoughts are nobody knows,

She sits with her secret hid, unguessed,
With her strange eyes bent on the distant west,
So the slow years come, and the slow year goes,
O'er the Lady Cecile.

Forty years! and June the third
Came with a storm—loud the winds did blow—
And up in her tower the lady heard
The deep waves calling her far below:
Wild they leaped and surged, wild the winds did blow,
And, listening alone, she thought she heard
"Cecile! Cecile!"

And, wrapping her cloak round her withered form,
She crept down the stairs of crumbling stone:
Higher and fiercer raged the storm
As she bent and plucked the rose—but one
Had the tempest spared—and the winds did moan,
And she thought that she heard o'er the voice of the storm,
"Cecile! Cecile!"

She placed the rose on her bloodless breast,
And dizzy and faint she reached the tower,
And her strange eyes looked out again on the west,
And a wave dashed up, as she looked from the tower,
Like a hand, and lifted the roots of the flower,
And swept it—carried it out to the west,
From the Lady Cecile.

And like death was her face, when suddenly,
  Strangely—a tremulous golden gleam
Pierced the pile of clouds, high-massed and gray,
  And the shining, quivering, golden beam
  Seemed a bridge of light—a gold highway
Thrown o'er the wild waves of the bay ;
                    And the Lady Cecile

Did eagerly out of her lattice lean
  With her glad eyes bent on that bridge gold-bright,
As if some form by her rapt eyes seen,
  Were beckoning her down that path of light,
  That quivering, shining, led from sight,
Ending afar in the sunset sheen.
                    And the Lady Cecile

Cried with her lips that erst were dumb
  "See! am I not true? your flower I wore,"
And her thin hand eagerly touched the flower,
  "He is smiling upon me! yes, love, I come."
  And a pleasant light, like the light of home,
Lit her eyes, and life and pain were o'er
                    To the Lady Cecile.

HOME.

A spirit is out to-night!
  His steeds are the winds : oh, list.
How he madly sweeps o'er the clouds.
  And scatters the driving mist.

We will let the curtains fall
  Between us and the storm ;
Wheel the sofa up to the hearth.
  Where the fire is glowing warm.

Little student, leave your book.
  And come and sit by my side :
If you dote on Tennyson so,
  I'll be jealous of him, my bride.

There, now I can call you my own!
  Let me push back the curls from your brow.
And look in your dark eyes and see
  What my bird is thinking of now.

Is she thinking of some high perch
  Of freedom, and lofty flight?
You smile ; oh, little wild bird.
  You are hopelessly bound to-night!

You are bound with a golden ring.
　　And your captor, like some grim knight,
Will lock you up in the deepest cell
　　Of his heart, and hide you from sight.

Sweetheart, sweetheart, do you hear far away
　　The mournful voice of the sea?
It is telling me of the time
　　When I thought you were lost to me.

Nay, love, do not look so sad;
　　It is over, the doubt and the pain;
Hark! sweet, to the song of the fire,
　　And the whisper of the rain.

STEPS WE CLIMB.

I.

Like idle clouds our lives move on,
By change and chance as idly blown ;
Our hopes like netted sparrows fly,
And vainly beat their wings and die.
Fate conquers all with stony will,
Oh, heart, be still—be still !

II.

No ! change and chance are slaves that wait
On Him who guides the clouds, not fate,
But the High King rules sea and sun,
He conquers, He, the Mighty One.
So powerless, 'neath that changeless will,
Oh, heart, be still—be still !

III.

As a young bird fallen from its nest
Beats wildly the kind hand against
That lifts it up, so tremblingly
Our hearts lie in God's hand, as He

Uplifts them by His loving will,
Oh, heart, be still—be still !

IV.

Uplifts them to a perfect peace,
A rest beyond all earthly ease,
'Neath the white shadow of the throne—
Low nest forever overshone
By tenderest love, our Lord's dear will ;
Oh, heart, be still—be still !

SQUIRE PERCY'S PRIDE.

THE Squire was none of your common men
  Whose ancestors nobody knows.
But visible was his lineage
  In the lines of his Roman nose,
That turned in the true patrician curve—
  In the curl of his princely lips,
In his slightly insolent eyelids,
  In his pointed finger-tips.

Very erect and grand looked the Squire
  As he walked o'er his broad estate,
For he felt that the earth was honored
  In bearing his honorable weight;
Proudly he strolled through his wooded park
  Deer-haunted and gloomily grand,
Or gazed from his pillared porticoes
  On his far-outlying land.

In a tiny whitewashed cottage,
  Half-covered with roses wild,
His cheerful-faced old gardener dwelt
  Alone with his motherless child ;

The Squire owned the very floor he trod,
  The grass in his garden lot,
The poor man had only this one little lamb
  Yet he envied the rich man not.

Poor was the gardener, yet rich withal
  In this priceless pearl of a girl,
So perfect a form, so faultless a face
  Never brightened the halls of an Earl;
Her eyes were two fathomless stars of light,
  And they shone on the Squire day by day,
Till their warm and perilous splendor
  So melted his pride away,

That he fain would have taken this pretty pet lamb
  To dwell in his stately fold,
To fetter it fast with a jeweled chain,
  And cage it with bars of gold:
But this coy little lamb loved its freedom,
  Not so free was she, though, to be true,
But, oh, the dainty and shy little lamb
  Well her master's voice she knew.

'Twas vain for the Squire the story to tell
  Of his riches and high descent,
As it fell into one rosy shell of an ear
  Out of its mate it went;

How one grim old ancestor into the land
  With William the Conqueror came,
She thought, the sweet, of a conqueror
  She knew with that very name.

So in this tender conflict
  The great man was forced to yield
To the handsome, sunburnt ploughman
  Who sowed and reaped in his field ;
For vainly he poured out his glittering gifts,
  Vainly he plead and besought,
Her heart was a tender and soft little heart,
  But it was not a heart to be bought.

So strange a thing I warrant you
  Happens not every day,
That the pride that had thriven for centuries
  One slight little maiden should slay ;
Why the proud Squire's Roman features
  Quivered and burned with shame,
And the picture of his grim ancestor
  Blushed in its antique frame.

Were this a romance, an idle tale,
  The Squire would sicken and die,
Slain by the pitiless cruelty,
  Of her dark and dazzling eye ;

And she in some shadowy convent
  Would bow her beautiful head,
But the hand that should have told penitent beads
  Wore a plain gold ring instead.

And he, not twice had his oak trees bloomed
  Ere he wedded a lady grand,
Whose tall and towering family tree,
  Had for ages darkened the land ;
'Twas a famous genealogical tree,
  With no modernly thrifty shoots,
But a tree with a sap of royalty
  Encrusting its mossy old roots.

This leaf he plucked from the outmost twig
  Was somewhat withered, 'tis true,
Long years had flown since it lightly danced
  To the summer air and the dew ;
Not much of a dowry brought she,
  In beauty or vulgar pelf,
But she had two or three ancestors
  More than the Squire himself.

'Twas much to muse o'er their musty names,
  And to think that his children's brains
Should be moved by the sanguine current,
  That had flown through such ancient veins ;

But I think, sometimes, in his secret heart,
    The Squire breathed woful sighs
For the fresh sweet face of the little maid,
    With the dark and wonderful eyes.

But she, no bird ever sang such songs
    To its mate from contented nest,
As this wee waiting wife, when the twilight
    Was treading the glorious west;
As she looked through the clustering roses,
    For the manly form that would come
Up through the cool green evening fields
    To this sweet little wife and home.

She could see the great stone mansion
    Towering over the oaks' dark green,
And the lawn like emerald velvet,
    Fit for the feet of a queen;
But round this brown-eyed princess,
    Did Love his ermine fold,
Queen was she of a richer realm,
    She had dearer wealth than gold.

ROSES OF JUNE.

She sat in the cottage door, and the fair June moon looked
    down
  On a face as pure as its own, an innocent face and sweet
  As the roses dewy white that grow so thick at her feet,
White, royal roses, fit for a monarch's crown.

And one is clasped in her slender hand, and one on her
    bosom lies,
  And two rare blushing buds loop up her light brown hair.
  Ah, roses of June, you never looked on a face so white
    and fair,
Such perfectly moulded lips, such sweet and heavenly eyes.

This low-walled home is dear to her, she has come to it
    to-day
  From the lordly groves of her palace home afar,
  But not to stay; there's a light on her brow like the light
    of a star,
And her eyes are looking beyond the earth, far, far away.

She was born in this cottage home, the sweetest rosebud of
    spring,

And grew with its flowers, the fairest blossom of all,
Till her friends ambitiously said she would grace the
kingliest hall,
And flattery breathed on her ear its passionate whispering.

A man of riches and taste saw the maiden's face,
And thought her beauty would grace his stately southern
home,
So he took her there, with pictures from France, and
statues from Rome,
And marvellous works of art from many an ancient place.

He decked her in costly attire, and showed her beauty with
pride,
As for sympathy and love, what need of these had she?
He had placed her amidst the choicest treasures of land
and sea,
His marble Hebe never complained, and why should his
bride?

He had polished the beautiful unknown gem and set it in
gold,
He had given her his name and his wealth, what more
could she ask?
When all other gifts were hers, it were surely an easy
task
Her pleading spirit's restless wings to fold.

The wise world called her blest, so heart be still,
    She had beauty, and splendor, and youth, and a husband
        calmly kind,
    And crowds of flattering friends her lofty mansion lined,
And dark-browed slaves awaited her queenly will.

Why should she dream of the past, of the days of old,
    Of her childhood home, and more oft of the home of the
        dead,
    Of the grave where she went alone the night before she
        was wed,
And knelt, with her pure cheek pressed to the marble cold !

It was not sin, she said, that those eyes of darkest blue
    Haunted her dreams more wildly from day to day,
    Since they looked on Heaven now, and she was so far
        away,
She could love the dead and still be to the living true.

She could think of him, the one who loved her best,
    Of him who true had been if all the world deceived,
    Who felt all grief with her when she was grieved,
And shared each joy that thrilled her girlish breast.

It was not sin that she heard that voice, gentle and deep,
    And the echo of a name—it was cut in marble now—
    So it was not sin, she said, as she breathed it low
In the midnight hour when all but she were asleep.

But she wearier grew of pride and pomp, like a homesick
    child she pined,
  And paler grew her cheek, as worn with a wearing pain.
  She said the fresh free country air would seem so sweet
    again,
So she went to her childhood home, as a pilgrim goes to a
    shrine,

And she looked down the orchard path and the meadow's
    clover bloom ;
  She stood by the stone-walled well that had mirrored her
    face when a child,
  She saw where the robins built, and her roses clambered
    wild,
And lingered lost in thought in each low and rustic room.

And she sat in the cottage door while the fair June moon
    looked down
  On a face as pure as its own, an innocent face, and sweet
  As the roses wet with dew that grew so thick at her feet,
White, royal roses, fit for a monarch's crown.

But at night, when silence and sleep on the lonely hamlet fell
  Like a spirit clad in white through the graveyard gate she
    passed,
  And the stars bent down to hear, " I have come to you,
    love, at last,"
While through the valley solemnly sounded the midnight bell.

And her southern birds will wait her coming in vain,
  Their starry eyes impatiently pierce the palm-trees' shade,
  And her roses droop in their bowers, alone they'll wither
      and fade.
Roses of June you are gone, but we know you will blossom
      again.

MAGDALENA.

Who falsely called thee destroyer, still white Angel of Death?
    Oh not a destroyer here, but a kind restorer, thou,
For the guilty look is gone, died out with her failing breath,
    And the sinless peace of a babe has come to lip and brow.

Drowned in the heaving tide with her life, is her burden of
      woe,
    The dreary weight of sin, the woeful, troublesome years,
The cold pure touch of the water has washed the shame
      from her brow
    Leaving a calm immortal, that looks like the chrism of peace.

I fancy her smile was like this, as she pulled at her mother's
      gown
    Drawing her out with childish fingers to watch the red of
      the skies
On the old brown doorstep of home, while the peaceful sun
      went down,
    With her mother's hand on her brow, and the glow of the
      west in her eyes.

" An outcast vile and lost," you say, yes, she went astray,
    Astray, when the crimson wine of life ran fresh and wild,

With mother's tender hand no more on her brow, put away
   The grasses beneath, and she was alone and almost a child.

Like a kid decoyed to its death, the stealthy panther lures.
   Mocking the voice of its dam, thus he led the innocent
      child
Through her tenderness down to ruin, he is a friend of yours,
   And admired by all ; as you say, "men will be wild."

But I wonder if God, so far above on His great white throne
   The clanging tumult of trouble and doubt that mortals vex ;
When the murmur of a crime sweeps up from earth with
      woeful moan,
   If He pauses, ere He condemns, to ask the offender's sex.

And if so, whether the weaker or stronger He blames the
      most,
   The tempter or tempted a tithe of His tender compassion
      claims,
Whether the selfish or too unselfish, those who through love
      or lust are lost,
   He in His infinite wisdom and mercy most condemns.

Frown not, I know her evil our womanly nature shuns,
   Turns from, with shuddering horror ; but now so low is
      her head
For God's sake, woman, remember your own little ones
   Lying safely at home in their snow-white sheltered bed.

Your own little girls, for them does the flame of your anger
    burn,
  " Such creatures will draw down innocence into guilt and
    woe."
I think from eternity vast she will scarcely return
    To entice them to sin, you can safely forgive her now.

" You will not countenance wrong, but fiercely war for the
    right
  Even unto the bitter death." Very good, you should do so,
But, my friend, if your own secret thought had blossomed to
    light
  In temptation, you might have been in this outcast's place,
    you know.

So let us be pitiful, grateful that God's strong hand
  Has held our own, and the tale of a woman's despair
And penitent sin, He stooped and wrote in the perishing
    sand ;
  We carve the record in stone, weak, sinful souls that we
    are.

In the arms of the kind all-mother, but close to the sorrow-
    ful wave,
  With its voice no longer moaning to her a despairing call,
But a dirge deploring and deep ; we will make her grave,
  With healing grasses above her, and God over all.

MY ANGEL.

Last night she came unto me,
  And kneeling by my side,
Laid her head upon my bosom,
  My beautiful, my bride ;
My lost one, with her soft dark eyes,
  And waves of sunny hair.
I smoothed the shining tresses,
With tearful, fond caresses,
  And words of thankful prayer.

And then a thrill of doubt and pain,
  My jealous heart swept o'er ;
We were parted—she was dwelling
  Upon a far-off shore ;
Yet He who made my sad heart, knew
  I loved her more and more ;
My love more true and perfect grew,
  As each dark day passed o'er ;
But she whose heart had been my own,
  Who loved me tenderly,
Whose last low words I knelt to hear,
  Were, " How can I leave thee ?"

And " Death would seem as sweet as life,
    Could we together be."
Now, though we two were parted
    By such a distance wide,
By such a strange and viewless realm,
    By such a boundless tide,
Her gentle face was radiant
    With a surpassing bliss ;
She was happier in that distant land,
    Than she ever was in this,
And in some other tenderness,
    Some other love divine,
She had found a peace and happiness,
    She never found in mine.

So with a tender chiding,
    I could not quite suppress,
Though well my darling knew
    I would not make her pleasures less.
" Are you happy, love ?" I said,
    " Are you happy, love, without me ?"
Then she raised her gentle head,
    And twined her arms about me ;
Yet while my tears fell faster,
    Beneath her mute caress,
Her face had all the glory
    Of a sainted soul at rest ;

And her voice was sweet as music,
  " I am happy—I am blest."

" Do you know how lonely-hearted
  I have been each weary day,
Praying that each passing hour
  Would bear my life away,
That we might be united
  Upon that distant shore ?"

" Laurence, we are not parted,
  I am with you evermore."

" I cannot see you, darling,
  Your face I cannot see."

" Can you see the moon's white fingers,
  That leads the pleading sea ?
Can you see the fragrance lingering
  Where summer roses be ?
The soft winds tender clasping,
  The close-enwrapping air
Enfolding you—Oh, Laurence,
  I am with you everywhere."

Then while her face grew brighter
  As with a heavenly glow,

In tenderness unspeakable.
   She kissed my lips and brow ;
Then I lost her—then she left me,
   As at the set of day
The snowy clouds float outward,
   And melt in light away.
I heard low strains of melody
   No earthly choir could sing,
A light breath floated past me,
   As from a gliding wing ;
And on my darkened spirit
   There fell so bright a gleam,
I knew the blessed vision
   Was not in truth a dream ;
Though death had won from my embrace,
   My beautiful, my bride,
I had won a richer treasure,
   An angel by my side.

The Father careth for us all
   In pity, and I know
My love is not forever gone
   From him who loved her so ;
When a few more days have drifted
   Their shadows over me,
When the golden gates are lifted,
   My angel I shall see ;

Her veiled face in its glory
  Upon my gaze will rise,
And Heaven will shine upon me
  Through the sweetness of her eyes.

GRIEF.

WHAT though the Eden morns were sweet with song
  Passing all sweetness that our thought can reach ;
Crushing its flowers noon's chariot moved along
  In brightness far transcending mortal speech ;
Yet in the twilight shades did God appear,
Oh welcome shadows so that He draw near.

Prosperity is flushed with Papal ease
  And grants indulgences to pride of word,
Robing our soul in pomp and vanities,
  Ah! no fit dwelling for our gentle Lord ;
Grief rends those draperies of pride and sin,
And so our Lord will deign to enter in.

Then carefully we curb each thought of wrong,
  We walk more softly, with more reverent feet—
As in His presence chamber, hush our tongue,
  And in the holy quiet, solemn, sweet,
We feel His smile, we hear His voice so low,
So we can bless Him that He gave us woe.

What cares the sailor in the sheltered cove
  For the past peril of the stormy sea :

Dear from grief's storm the haven of His love,
  And so He bringeth us where we would be ;
We trust in Him, we lean upon His breast,
Who shall make trouble when He giveth rest?

WILD OATS.

On gay young husbandmen would you be sure of a crop
  Upspringing rankly, an abundant and bountiful yield?
  Go forth in the morning, and sow on your life's broad field
This pleasantly odorous seed, then smooth the ground on top,
  Or leave it rough, with the utmost undeceit,
Never you fear, it will thriftily thrive and grow,
  Loading the harvest plain beneath your feet,
With the ripened sheaves of shame, remorse, and woe.

You have but to sow the seed, no care will it want,
  For he who soweth tares while the husbandman sleeps
  Taketh unwearied pains, a vigilant guard he keeps
Tirelessly watching, and tending each evil plant.
These are his pleasure gardens, leased to him through time
  Where he walketh to and fro, chanting a demon song:
  Tending with ghastly fingers, the scarlet buds of wrong.
And drinking greedily in the sweet perfume of crime.

And of all the seeds, the one that thriftiest thrives
  Is the color of ruby wine, when it flashes high—
  Who would think the tiny seed so fair to the eye
Could cast such a deadly shade over countless lives,

And branch out into murder in one springing shoot ;
  Thrifty branches of sin, bristling with thorns of woe
  Shadowing graves where broken hearts lie low,
And minds that were God-like lowered beneath the brute.

AUTUMN.

How the sumac banners bent, dripping as if with blood,
  What a mournful presence brooded upon the slumbrous
    air;
A mocking-bird screamed noisily in the depths of the
    silent wood,
  And in my heart was crying the raven of despair,
Thrilling my being through with its bitter, bitter cry—
" It were better to die, it were better to die."

For she, my love, my fate, she sat by my side
  On a fallen oak, her cheek all flushed with a bashful
    shame,
Telling me what her innocent heart had hid—
  " For was not I her brother, her dear brother, all but in
    name."
I listened to her low words, but turned my face away—
Away from her eyes' soft light, and the mocking light of the
    day.

" He was noble and proud," she said, " and had chosen her
    from all
  The haughty ladies, and great; she didn't deserve her lot."

I knew her peer could never be found in palace or hall,
　And my white face told my thought, but she saw it not.
She was crushing some scarlet leaves in her dainty fingers
　　　of snow,
Her maiden joy crowning her face with a radiant glow.

"She had wanted me to know," and then a smile and a
　　　blush ;
　Her smile was always just like a baby's smile, and the red
Came to her cheek at a word or a glance—then there fell
　　　a hush.
　She was waiting some word from me, I knew, so I said,
" May Heaven bless you both "—words spoken full quietly,
And she, God bless her, never knew how much they cost
　　　to me.

How the sumac banners bent, dripping as if with blood,
　What a mournful presence brooded upon the slumbrous
　　　air ;
A mocking-bird screamed noisily in the depths of the silent
　　　wood,
　And in my heart was crying the raven of despair,
Thrilling my being through with its desolate, desolate cry—
" It were better to die, it were better to die."

The white dawn follows the darkness; out of the years' decay
　Shineth the golden fire that gildeth the autumn with
　　　light ;

From another's sin and loss, cometh this good to me,
  By another's fall am I raised to this blissful height.
" Let me be humble," said my heart, as from her sweet lips
    fell,
" Let a prayer for him arise, with the sound of our marriage
    bell."

THE FAIREST LAND.

'Twas a bleak dull moor that stretched before
The low stone porch of the cottage door,
And standing there was a youth and maid,
He for long journeying seemed arrayed,
And the sunset flamed in the burnished west,
And a proud throb beat in the young man's breast,
As he whispered, " Sweet, will you come to me
In that fairer land beyond the sea ?"

" The wonderful western land ; in dreams
I have seen its prairies green, and gleams
Of its shining waterfalls, valleys fair,
And a voice in my dreams has called me there
Where man is a man, and not a clod,
And must bend the knee to none but God.
A home will I make for thee and me
In that fairer land beyond the sea."

" But the cruel sea where the fated ships
Go down to their doom"— But he kissed the lips—
The trembling lips, till they smiled again,
And his bright hopes cheered her heart's dull pain,

And she laid her head on his hopeful breast,
And looked with him to the glowing west,
And said, " I will come, I will come to thee
To that fairer land beyond the sea."

And the crimson light changed to daffodil—
To ashen gray, but they stood there still,
And high o'er the west shone the evening star
As still he pictured that home afar—
" The peace and the bliss our own at last
When this dreary parting all is past,
When my heart's dear love, you come to me
In that fairer land beyond the sea."

So he sailed ; but saddest 'tis alway
Not for those who go, but for those who stay ;
And her sweet eyes gathered a shadow dim
As days went by with no news of him,
And weeks and months, but at last it came,
As the gray moor shone with the sunset flame
Her quick eyes glanced the strange lines o'er,
Then she fell like dead on the cottage floor.

'Twas a stranded ship on a rocky coast,
One true heart brave, when hope was lost,
How he toiled till all the shore had gained,
And only a baby form remained

On ship, how he breasted the surging tide
With Death a-wrestling side by side,
How he lifted the child to its mother's knee,
As a great wave washed him out to sea.

And for days the maid in the cottage door
Sat and looked o'er the dreary moor,
Her cheeks grew white 'neath her blinding tears,
And the sunset rays seemed cruel spears
That pierced her heart; and ashen gray
Turned the earth and sky, the night, the day;
But at last a star shone high above—
The tender star of the heavenly love.

For as her life ebbed day by day,
The High Countrie, the Fair alway,
Rose 'fore her eyes, the safe, sweet home,
And she seemed to hear, "Love, will you come?"
And so one eve when a bridge of gold
Seemed spanning the last sea dim and cold,
She went to him, for aye to be
In the Fairest land beyond the sea.

THE MESSENGER.

Is his form hidden by some cliff or crag,
　Or does he loiter on the shelving shore ?
We know not, though we know he waits for us,
　Somewhere upon the road that lies before.

And when he bids us we must follow him,
　Must leave our half-drawn nets, our houses, lands,
And those we love the most, and best, ah they
　In vain will cling to us with pleading hands !

He will not wait for us to gird our robes,
　And be they white as saints, or soiled and dim,
We can but gather them around our form,
　And take his icy hand and follow him.

Oh ! will our palm cling to another palm,
　Loath, loath to loose our hold of love's warm grasp.
Or shall we free our hand from the hand of grief,
　And reach it gladly out to meet his clasp ?

Sometimes I marvel when we two shall meet,
　When I shall hear that stealthy step, and see
The unseen form that haunteth mortal dreams,
　The stern-browed face, the eyes of mystery.

Shall I be waiting for some wished-for wealth,
  Impatient, by the shore of a purple sea?
But when the vessel's keel grates on the sand,
  Will *he* lean down its side and call to me?

Shall I in thymy pastures cool and sweet
  See the lark soaring through the rosy air?
Ah, then, will his dark face look down on me,
  'Neath the white splendor of the morning star?

Shall I be resting from the noonday blaze,
  In the rich summer of a blossoming land,
And idly glancing through the lotus leaves,
  Behold the shadow of his beckoning hand?

Or in some inland village, shaded deep,
  With silence brooding o'er the quiet place,
Shall I look from some lattice crowned with flowers,
  In the calm twilight and behold his face?

Or shall I over such a lonely way,
  Beset with fears, my weary footsteps wend,
So desolate, that I shall greet his face
  With joy as a desired and welcome friend?

Oh, little matters it when we shall meet,
  Upon the quiet shore, or on the sea,
If he shall lead us to the golden gate,
  Dear Lord, if he shall lead us unto Thee.

SLEEP.

COME, gentle sleep, with the holy night,
  Come with the stars and the white moonbeams,
Come with your train of handmaids bright,
  Blessed and beautiful dreams.

Bring the exile to his home again,
  Let him catch the gleam of its low white wall :
Let his wife cling to his neck and weep,
  And his children come at their father's call.

Give to the mother the child she lost,
  Laid from her heart to a clay-cold bed ;
Let its breath float over her tear-wet cheek,
  And her cold heart warm 'neath its bright young head.

Take the sinner's hand and lead him back
  To his sinless youth and his mother's knee ;
Let him kneel again 'neath her tender look,
  And murmur the prayer of his infancy.

Lead the aged into that wondrous clime,
  Home of their youth and land of their bliss ;
Let them forget in that beautiful world,
  The sin and the sorrow of this.

And gently lead my love, my own,
 Tenderly clasp her snow-white hand,
Wrap her in garments of soft repose,
 And lead her into your mystic land.

Let your fairest handmaids bow at her feet,
 Her path o'er your loveliest roses be ;
And let all the flowers with their perfumed lips
 Whisper of me—of me.

Come, gentle sleep, with the holy night,
 Come with the stars and the white moonbeams,
Come with your train of handmaids bright,
 Blessed and beautiful dreams.

THE SONG OF THE SIREN.

Oh, I am the siren, the siren of the sea,
  The sea, the wondrous sea, that lies forevermore before :
I stand a fairy shape upon the shadow of a cliff
  Where the water's drowsy ripple laps the phantom of a
      shore,
And, oh, so fair, so fair am I, I draw all hearts to me.
For I am the siren, the siren of the sea.

All the glory of my golden tresses gleams upon the air,
  How it falls about my snowy shoulders, round and bare
    and white ;
My lips are full of love as rounded grapes are full of
  wine,
  And my eyes are large and languid, and full of dewy
    light ;
Oh, I lure the idle landsmen many a league for love of me,
For I am the siren, the siren of the sea.

Sometimes they press so near that my breath is on their
  cheek,
  And their eager hands can almost touch the glowing bowl
    I bear,

They can see the beaded froth, the ruby glitter of the wine,
  Then I slip from their embraces like a breath of summer
     air ;
Oh, I lightly, lightly glide away, they come no nigher me,
For I am the siren, the siren of the sea.

Sometimes I float along a-standing in a boat,
  Before the ships becalmed, where dusky sailors stand,
And the helmsman drops his oar, and the lookout leaves his
     glass,
  So I beckon them, and lure them, with the whiteness of
     my hand ;
Oh, this the song I sing, well they listen unto me !
For I am the siren, the siren of the sea.

    Would you from toil and labor flee,
    Oh float ye out on this wonderful sea,
    From islands of spice the zephyrs blow,
    Swaying the galleys to and fro ;
    Silken sails and a balmy breeze
    Shall waft you unto a perfect ease.

    Fold your hands and rest, and rest,
    The sun sails on from the east to the west,
    The days will come, and the days will go,
    What good can man for his labor show
    In passionless peace, come float with me
    Over the waves of this wonderful sea.

Would you forget, oh sorrowful soul,
Come and drink of this golden bowl,
With jewelled poppies about the rim,
Drink of the wine that flushes its brim,
And drown all your haunting memories there,
Your woe and your weary care.

Oh, I am the siren, the siren of the sea,
   The sea, the wondrous sea, that lies forevermore before ;
Oh, the mystic music ripples, how they break in rosy spray,
   But the crystal wave will mock them, they will reach it
      nevermore,
For it glides away, I glide away, they come no nigher me,
For I am the siren, the siren of the sea.

EIGHTEEN SIXTY-TWO.

I.

THERE's a tear in your eye, little Sybil,
　　Gathering large and slow ;
Oh, Sybil, sweet little Sybil,
　　What are you thinking of now ?

Push back the velvet curtains
　　That darken the lonely room,
For shadows peer out of their crimson depths,
　　And the statues gleam white in the gloom.

How the cannons' thunder rolls along,
　　And shakes the lattice and wall,
Oh, Sybil, sweet little Sybil,
　　What if your father should fall ?

The smoky clouds sweep up from the field
　　And darken the earth and sea.
" God save him ! God save him!"
　　Wherever he may be.

II.

Oh, pretty dark-eyed bird of the South,
    With your face so mournful and white
There is many a little Northern girl
    That is breathing that prayer to-night.

There's a little girl on the hills of Maine
    Looking out through the fading light,
She looks down the winding path, and says,
    " He will surely come to-night !"

The table is set, the lamp is trimmed,
    The fire has a ruddy glow
That streams like a beacon down the path,
    To the dusky valley below.

There is smiling hope on the pretty face
    Pressed so close to the pane,
And her eyes are like blue violets
    After a summer rain.

III.

How you tremble, little Sybil,
    At the cannons' dreadful sound,
Did you see far away, the fallen steed,
    And its rider prone on the ground ?

The dark brown locks so low in the dust,
  The scarf with a crimson stain—
Oh, Sybil, poor little Sybil,
  He will not come back again.

IV.

Right gallantly and well he fought
  Hand to hand with as brave a foe,
Their faces hid by the nodding plumes,
  And the dense clouds hanging low.

Did they think, these hot-blooded captains,
  That Death was so close by their side,
When Howard has fallen, the bravest—
  Rung out on the air far and wide.

" Howard ?"   His foeman kneels by his side,
  And raises his head to his knee—
Oh, God ! that brothers should part in youth,
  And thus should their meeting be.

Unheard is the deafening battle roar,
  Unseen is that dying look ;
He hears but the sound of a childish laugh,
  And the song of a Northern brook.

He sees two white forms kneeling
  In the twilight sweet and dim,
One low couch angel-guarded,
  By a mother's evening hymn.

v.

The Angel of Death came down with the night,
  Came down with the gathering gloom ;
God pity the little dark-eyed girl,
  Alone in the lonely room.

But still by his side his brother kneels,
  Chill horror has frozen his veins ;
He heeds not the glancing shower of shells,
  That with red fire glitters and rains.

And he heeds not the fiery cavalry charge,
  That sweeps like a billow on
To death, oh, the bravest and saddest sight,
  That man ever gazed upon !

The last shot ! What is one life
  To the battle's gory gain ?
But, alas, for the little blue-eyed maid
  Away on the hills of Maine !

AWEARY.

THE clouds that vex the upper deep
 Stay not the white sail of the moon;
And lips may moan, and hearts may weep,
 The sad old earth goes rolling on.

O'er smiling vale, and sighing lake,
 One shadow cold is overthrown:
And souls may faint, and hearts may break,
 The sad old earth goes rolling on.

TOO LOW.

" My house is thatched with violet leaves
    And paved with daisies fine,
Scarlet berries droop over its eaves,
    Tall grasses round it shine ;
With softest down I have lined my nest,
Securely now will I sit and rest.

" When their wings break from their silvery shell,
    Touched by my tender care,
Here shall my little ones safely dwell.
    Little ones soft and fair ;
Some summer morn they shall try their wings
While their father sits by my side and sings."

Hard by, just over the streamlet's edge
    A great rock towered in might,
High up, half hidden in moss and sedge,
    Were safe little nooks and bright ;
Ah well for the bird with her tender breast,
Had she flown to the rock to build her nest !

Poor bird, she built her nest too low ;
    Alas ! for the bird, alas !

That she chose that spot to her woe
 In the low dewy grass ;
For the reaper came with his gleaming blade.
Alas for love in the violet shade !

AT LAST.

What though upon a wintry sea our life bark sails,
What though we tremble 'neath its cruel gales,
      Its icy blast;
We see a happy port lie far before,
We see its shining waves, its sunny shore,
Where we shall wander, and forget the troubled past,
      At last.

No storms approach that quiet shore, no night
Falls on its silver streams, and valleys bright,
      And gardens vast;
Within that pleasant land of perfect peace
Our toil-worn feet shall stay, our wanderings cease;
There shall we, resting, all forget the past,
      At last.

The sorrows we have hid in silent weariness,
As birds above a wounded, bleeding breast,
      Their bright plumes cast;
The griefs like mourners in a dark array,
That haunt our footsteps here, will flee away,
And leave us to forget the sorrowful past,
      At last.

Voices we loved sound from those far-off lands,
And thrill our hearts; life's golden sands
   Are dropping fast ;
Soon shall we meet by the river of peace, and say,
As the night flees before the eye of day,
So faded from our eyes the mournful past,
   At last.

TWILIGHT.

DRAPED in shadows stands the mountain
    Against the eastern sky,
Above it the fair summer moon
    Looks downward tenderly ;
And Venus in the glowing west,
    Opens her languid eye.

Now the winds breathe softer music,
    Half a song, and half a sigh ;
While twilight wraps her purple veil
    Around us silently,
And our thoughts appear like pictures,
    Pictures shaded wondrously.

Quiet landscapes, sweet and lonely,
    Silvery sea, and shadowy glade,
Forest lakes by man forsaken,
    Where the white fawn's steps are stayed :
And contadinos straying
    'Neath the Pantheon's solemn shade.

And we see the wave bridged over
    By the moonlight's mystic link,

Desert wells by tall palms shaded,
  Where dusky camels drink ;
While dark-eyed Arab maidens
  Fill their pitchers at the brink.

And secluded convent chapels,
  Where veiled nuns kneel to pray,
With a dim light streaming o'er them
  Through arches quaint and gray,
While down the long and winding aisles
  Low music dies away.

There is a starry twilight
  Of the soul, as sadly fair,
When our wild emotions are at rest,
  Like the pale nuns at prayer;
And our griefs are hushed like sleepers,
  And put off the robes of care.

THE SEWING-GIRL.

I ASKED to see the dead man's face,
   As I gave the servant my well-filled basket;
And she deigned to lead me, a wondrous grace,
   Where he lay asleep in his rosewood casket.
I was only the sewing-girl, and he the heir to this princely
      palace.
   Flowers, white flowers, everywhere,
In odorous cross, and anchor, and chalice.
   The smallest leaf might touch his hair;
But I—my God! I must stand apart,
With my hands pressed silently on my heart,
I must not touch the least brown curl;
For I was only the sewing-girl.

If his stately mother knew what I know,
   As she weeping stood by his side this morning.
Would she clasp me in motherly love and woe—
   Or drive me out in the cold with scorning?
If she knew that I loved him better than life,
   Better than death; since for him I gave
My hopes of rest, that I faced life's strife,
   And renounced the quiet and restful grave,

When his strong, true hand drew me back that day,
  When woe, and want, and the want of pity
Drove me down where the cold waves lay
  Like wolves round the walls of this cruel city.
" Not much ?" would she say with her proud lip's curl—
"Only the life of a sewing-girl ?"

No love for me in his heart did linger—
  I saw the lady, his promised bride,
I saw his ring on her slender finger,
  As she weeping stood by his mother's side.
That same ring shone, as he lifted me
  Dripping and cold from the sea-waves bitter.
I had thought Heaven's light I next should see,
  But earth's sun shone in its ruby glitter ;
I had thought when I looked in the Lord's mild face,
  That He would forgive my rashness and sin,
When He knew there was not a single place,
  Not a place so small that I could creep in.
And I wanted a home, and I longed for love,
And God and mother were both above.
But he showed me my sin, and taught me to live,
Above this life of tumult and whirl,
Though I was only a sewing-girl.

What shall I do with the life he won,
  From death that day, in a hard-won battle ?

Shall I lay it down e'er the rising sun
   Looks down on the city's roar and rattle?
Shall I lay it down e'er the midnight dim
With horrible shadows is roofed and paved?
   No, I will make it so pure and sweet,
That angels shall say with smiles to him,
   When we meet above on the golden street:
" Behold the soul of her you saved."
Maybe it shall add to his crown one pearl,
Though only the soul of a sewing-girl.

HARRY THE FIRST.

In his arm-chair, warmly cushioned,
In the quiet earned by labor,
Life's reposeful Indian summer,
Grandpa sits; and lets the paper
Lie upon his knee unheeded.
Shine his cheeks like winter apples,
Gleams his smile like autumn sunshine,
As he looks on little Harry,
First-born of the house of Graham,
Bravely cutting teeth in silence,
Cutting teeth with looks heroic.
Some deep thought seems moving Grandpa,
Ponders he awhile in silence,
Then he turns, and says to Grandma,
" Nancy, do you think that ever
There was such a child before?"

Grandma, with her prim precision
The seam-stitch impaleth deftly
On her sharp and glittering needle,
Then she turns and answers calmly,

With a deep assurance—" Never
Was there such a child before !"

Papa thinks so, but in manly
Dignity controls his feelings ;
More than half a year a father,
He must show a cool composure,
He must stately be if ever.
But his dark eyes plainly tell it,
Tell it, as he sayeth proudly,
" Papa's man is little Harry."

Mamma, maybe, does not speak it,
But she prints the thought on velvet,
Rosy-hued, with fondest kisses,
When the pink, soft page is lying
Folded closely to her bosom.

A little farther goes his auntie,
Aged fourteen—age of fancy ;
She looks down the future ages
With her wise, prophetic vision ;
Sees the babies pass before her,
Babies of the twentieth century,
All the long and dusty ages,
To the thousand years of glory.
Oh, the host of bright-eyed children,
Thronging like the stars at midnight,

Faces sweet and countless, as the
Rose-leaves of a thousand summers.
All the pretty heads so curly
That shall hold a riper wisdom
Than our youthful planet dreams of ;
All the ranks of dimpled shoulders,
That shall move Time's rolling chariot
Nearer to the golden city ;
Vieweth these the blue-eyed prophet,
Still the oracle says calmly,
Speaks the seer with golden tresses—
" No ! there never was, nor will be
Such a child as our Harry,
Such a noble boy as Harry."

Summer brings a wealth of flowers,
Flowers of every form and color,
Orange, crimson, royal purple,
All along the mountain passes,
All along the pleasant valley,
Low the emerald branches bendeth
With their weight of summer glory.

But they do not waken in us
Half the tender, blissful feeling,
Half the pure and sweet emotion
As the first spring-flower in April,

With its lashes tinged with crimson,
Partly raised from eyes half-timid,
Fearful that the snow will drown it;
How we love the dainty blossom,
How we wear it in our bosom.

Just so with the tree ancestral,
Many flowers may blossom on it,
But the first wee bud that's grafted,
To its heart, ah, how we love it ;
Others may be loved as fondly,
But they are not loved so proudly,
Loved so blindly, so entirely.

Yes, when first the heart's door opens
To the touch of baby fingers,
Quick the dimpled feet will bear them
To the dearest place and warmes⁺
Plenty room enough for other
Buds of beauty, buds of promise,
In the heart's capacious chambers ;
But the first is firmly settled—
Little Harry's firmly settled
In the centre of affection ;
Later ones must settle round him.

THE CRIMINAL'S BETROTHED.

As on a waveless sea, a vessel strikes
    Upon a treacherous rock ;
Waking the sailors from their happy dreams
    By the swift, terrible shock.

Dreaming of shaded village streets, and home,
    Forgetting the cruel sea
Till the shock came—so woke I, yet I know
    'Twas Love, I loved, not he.

'Tis not the star the wave so wildly clasps,
    Only its form reflected in the stream ;
'Tis not a broken heart I mourn,
    Only a broken dream.

I should have died when he was brought so low,
    Had it been him I loved,
Died clinging to him, as to the blasted oak
    The ivy clings unmoved.

'Twas Love that looked on me with strange, sweet eyes
    Burning with marvellous flame ;
Love was the idol that I worshipped, though
    I gave to it his name.

I gave to Love his name, his glance, his brow,
  His low-toned voice, his smile,
Oh, soul be patient ; I can sever them
  But yet a little while—

Before I put away these outward forms
  Deceiving, sweet disguises, which Love wore
Let my heart break into regretful tears
  Just once, and then no more.

Just once, as fond friends watch the fading sail
  Bearing away a guest of truest worth,
They give this little time to grief, and then
  Return to their desolate hearth,

And build new fires, and gather dewy flowers,
  Let the pure air into the vacant room,
So light, and bloom, and sweetness, all
  Shall penetrate its gloom.

I will be patient, in a little time
  Quiet, and full of rest,
God's peace will come, and, like a soft-winged bird,
  Settle upon my breast.

Not always thus shall beat my restless heart
  Like a wild eagle 'gainst its prison-bars ;
In some calm twilight of the future time
  I will sit, calm-browed, underneath the stars.

GONE BEFORE.

Fold the hands
Gently o'er the silent heart,
Soft palms nevermore to part
   From their quiet rest;
Ne'er to cling to broken reeds,
Plucking flowers to find them weeds ;
Ne'er to raise in anguished prayer,
Nor to clasp in wild despair
O'er a heart that bleeds ;
Softly o'er the peaceful breast,
   Fold the hands.

   Close the eyes ;
Loving eyes of softest blue,
Tender eyes of Heaven's own hue,
   Close in sleep.
Sleep thee, darling, through the night,
Dreaming fancies blest and bright,
Visions bathed in heavenly day,
Ne'er to fade and melt away
In the morning light ;
Dear eyes, nevermore to weep,
   Close in sleep.

Smooth the hair ;
Silken waves of sunny brown
Lay upon the white brow down,
Crowned with blossoms rare ;
Lilies on a golden stream,
Ne'er to fall in tendrils bright
On her shoulders bare and white ;
Ne'er to float in summer air
Wreathed with meadow daisies fair.
Lay away the broken crown
And your broken dream,
With one shining tress of hair,
Nevermore to need your care.

A WOMAN'S HEART.

My heart sings like a bird to-night
That flies to its nest in the soft twilight,
   And sings in its brooding bliss;
Ah! I so low, and he so high,
What could he find to love? I cry,
   Did ever love stoop so low as this?

As a miser jealously counts his gold,
I sit and dream of my wealth untold,
   From the curious world apart;
Too sacred my joy for another eye,
I treasure it tenderly, silently,
   And hide it away in my heart.

Dearer to me than the costliest crown
That ever on queenly forehead shone
   Is the kiss he left on my brow;
Would I change his smile for a royal gem?
His love for a monarch's diadem?
   Change it? Ah, no, ah, no!

My heart sings like a bird to-night
That flies away to its nest of light

To brood o'er its living bliss ;
Ah ! I so low, and he so high,
What could he find to love? I cry,
　　Did ever love stoop so low as this !

WARNING.

When enwrapped in rosy pleasure,
  Our careless pulses beat,
  With a rhythm sweet, sweet,
To the music's merry measure.

When world waves rise around us,
  With soft transparent weight,
  Light in seeming, yet so great,
The liquid chains have bound us.

Then softly downward falling,
  If we listen, we can hear,
  From a purer atmosphere,
A warning and a calling.

'Tis not uttered to our ear,
  To our spirit it is spoken,
  In the wonderful, unbroken
Heavenly speech that spirits hear.

Strange and solemn doth it roll
  Downward like a yearning cry,
  From that belfry far on high,
Warning, calling to our soul.

Ever, ever, doth it roll,
  Our angel guards the tower,
  Ringing, ringing, every hour,
Warning, calling to our soul.

GENIEVE TO HER LOVER.

I turn the key in this idle hour
  Of an ivory box, and looking, lo—
See only dust—the dust of a flower ;
  The waters will ebb, the waters will flow,
  And dreams will come, and dreams will go,
      Forever.

Oh, friend, if you and I should meet
  Beneath the boughs of the bending lime,
Should you in the same low voice repeat
  The tender words of the old love rhyme,
  It could not bring back the same old time,
      Never.

When you laid this rose against my brow,
  I was quite unused to the ways of men,
With my trusting heart ; I am wiser now,
  So I smile, remembering my heart-throbs then,
  The dust of a rose cannot blossom again,
      Never.

The brow that you praised has colder grown,
  And hearts will change, I suppose they must,

A rose to be lasting, should blossom in stone,
Ashes to ashes, dust to dust,
Dead are the rose, the love, and the trust,
Forever.

THE WILD ROSE.

In a waste of yellow sand, on the brow of a dreary hill,
  A slight little slip of a rose struggled up to the light,
The seed maybe was sown there by the south wind's idle
      will,
  But there it grew and blossomed, pale and white.
Only one flower it bore, and that was frail and small,
But I think it was brave to try to grow at all.

In groves of fair Cashmere, or sheltered garden of kings,
  Sweet with a thousand flowers, with birds of paradise
Fanning her blushing cheeks with their glowing wings,
  Praising her deepening bloom with their great bright
      eyes,
Life would have been a pleasure instead of a toil,
To my pale little patient rose of the sandy soil.

Did she ever sadly think of her wasted life,
  Folding her wan weak hands so helpless and still;
And the great oak by her sheltering glad bird life,
  And the thirsty meadows praising the running rill;
She could hear the happy work-day song of the busy brook.
While she, poor thing, could only stand and look.

Did the wee white rose ever think of her lonely life,
   That there were none to care if she tried to grow ;
None to care if the cloud that hung in the west
   Should burst, and scatter her pale leaves far and low !
Did she ever wish that the heavy cloud would fall
And hide her, so unblest, from the sight of all !

One sky bends o'er rich garden flowers, and those
   That dwell in barren soil, untended and unblest ;
And I think that God was pleased with the small white
      rose,
   That tried so patiently to live and do its best ;
That bravely kept its small leaves pure and fair
On the waste of dreary sand, and the desert air.

OUR BIRD.

She lay asleep, and her face shone white
   As under a snowy veil,
And the waxen hands clasped on her breast
   Were full of snowdrops pale;
But a holy calm touched the baby lips,
   The brow, and the sleeping eyes,
The look of an angel pitying us
   From the peace of Paradise.

And now though she lies 'neath the coffin-lid,
   We cannot think her dead;
But we think of her as of some delicate bird
   To a milder country fled.
'Twas a long, dark flight for our gentle dove,
   Our bird so tender and fair;
But we know she has reached the summer land
   And folded her white wings there.

THE TIME THAT IS TO BE.

I AM thinking of fern forests that once did towering stand,
Crowning all the barren mountains, shading all the dreary
land.

Oh, the dreadful, quiet brooding, the solitude sublime,
That reigned like shadowy spectres o'er the third great day
of time.

In long, low lines the tideless sea on dull gray shores did
break,
No song of bird, no gleam of wing, o'er wood or reedy
lake—

No flowers perfumed the pulseless air, no stars, no moon, no
sun
To tell in silver language, night was past, or day was done.

Only silence rising with the ghostly morning's misty light,
Silence, silence, settling down upon the moonless, starless
night.

And the ferns, and giant mosses, noiseless sentinels did stand,
Looking o'er the tideless ocean, watching o'er the dreary
    land.

Ferns gave place to glowing olives, and clusters dropping
    wine,
Mosses changed to oaken tissues, and cleft to fragrant pine.

Deft and noiseless fingers toiled, and wrought the great
    Creator's plan,
Through countless ages moulding earth for the abode of
    man.

Till each imperial day was bound by sunset's crimson bars,
The purple columns of the night crowned with the shining
    stars.

The ripe fruit seeks the sunlight through all the clustering
    leaves,
The earth is decked with golden maize, and costly yellow
    sheaves.

Countless silent centuries passed in fashioning good that
    doth appear,
Shall we weary and grow hopeless, waiting for the Golden
    Year?

    Thy kingdom come, in which Thy will is done,
      From myriad souls rises the yearning cry ;

Scatter palm-boughs—behold, a brighter sun
  Shall dawn in splendor, in a clearer sky ;
Upon the distant hills a glow we see,
That tells us of the Time that is to be.

The desert then shall blossom like the rose,
  The almond flourish on the rocky slopes :
Wisdom and beauty in rare union close,
  Making earth beautiful beyond our hopes.
High in the dusky east a star we see,
A herald of the Time that is to be.

The free-born soul shall not be captive then,
  Bound by decaying cords of narrow creeds,
God's image shall more clearly shine in men,
  Divinely shaped by holy aims and deeds.
Gleam, golden star, oh gleam o'er earth and sea,
A herald of the Time that is to be.

Fetters are broken, so the fern-leaves fall,
  A richer growth is budding, wondrous fair,
The flower of liberty shall bloom for all,
  And all shall breathe the healing of the air :
The blessed air that wraps a people free,
Within that glorious Time that is to be.

For what is slavery but woe and crime,
  And freedom is but liberty from these ;

Oh perfect hours, ye come, fair and sublime,
　　Bearing the sweet form of the baby, Peace,
Shine, golden star, oh shine o'er earth and sea,
A herald of the Time that is to be.

www.ingramcontent.com/pod-product-compliance
Lightning Source LLC
Chambersburg PA
CBHW030133030726
47498CB00007B/2685